The Path to the
Nest of Spiders

The Path to the Nest of Spiders
ITALO CALVINO

Translated from the Italian by Archibald Colquhoun

THE ECCO PRESS

New York

Il Sentiero Dei Nidi Di Ragno
Copyright © 1947 by Giulio Einaudi Editore, Torino
Preface Copyright © William Weaver, 1976
All rights reserved
Published in 1976 by The Ecco Press
1 West 30th Street, New York, N.Y. 10001
Published simultaneously in Canada by
The Macmillian Company of Canada Limited
Printed in the United States of America

Library of Congress Cataloging in Publication Data
Calvino, Italo.
   The path to the nest of spiders.
   Translation of Il sentiero dei nidi di ragno.
   Reprint of the 1957 ed. published by Beacon Press, Boston.
   I.   Title.
PZ3.C13956Pat10 [PQ4809.A45]   853′.9′14
ISBN 0-912-94631-8   76–5827

Preface

This was my first novel; I can almost say it was my first piece of writing, apart from a few stories. What impression does it make on me now, when I pick it up again? I read it not so much as something of mine but rather as a book born anonymously from the general atmosphere of a period, from a moral tension, a literary taste in which our generation recognized itself, at the end of World War II.

Italy's literary explosion in those years was less an artistic event than a physiological, existential, collective event. We had experienced the war, and we younger people—who had been barely old enough to join the partisans—did not feel crushed, defeated, "beat." On the contrary, we were victors, driven by the propulsive charge of the just-ended battle, the exclusive possessors of its heritage. Ours was not easy optimism, however, or gratuitous euphoria. Quite the opposite. What we felt we possessed was a sense of life as something that can begin again from scratch, a general concern with problems, even a capacity within us to survive torment and abandonment; but we added also an accent of bold gaiety. Many things grew out of that atmosphere, including the attitude of my first stories and my first novel.

This is what especially touches us today; the anonymous voice of that time, stronger than our still-uncertain individual inflections. Having emerged from an experience, a war and a civil war that had spared no one, made communication between the writer and his audience immediate. We were face to face, equals, filled with stories to tell; each had his own; each had lived an irregular, dramatic, adventurous life; we snatched the words from each other's mouths. With our renewed freedom of speech, all at first felt a rage to narrate: in the trains that were beginning to run again, crammed with people and sacks of flour and drums of olive oil, every passenger told his vicissitudes to strangers, and so did every customer at the tables of the cheap restaurants, every woman waiting in line outside a shop. The grayness of daily life seemed to belong to other periods; we moved in a varicolored universe of stories.

So anyone who started writing then found himself handling the same material as the nameless oral narrator. The stories we had personally enacted or had witnessed mingled with those we had already heard as tales, with a voice, an accent, a mimed expression. During the partisan war, stories just experienced were transformed and transfigured into tales told around the fire at night; they had already gained a style, a language, a sense of bravado, a search for anguished or grim effects. Some of my stories, some pages of this novel originated in that new-born oral tradition, in those events, in that language.

But . . . but the secret of how one wrote then did not lie only in this elementary universality of content; that was not its mainspring (perhaps having begun this preface by recalling a collective mood has made me forget I am speaking of a book, something written down, lines of words on the white page). On the contrary, it had never been so clear that the stories were raw material: the explosive charge of freedom that animated the young writer was not so much his wish to document or to inform as it was his desire to *express*. Express what? Ourselves, the harsh flavor of life we had just learned, so many things we thought we knew or were, and perhaps really knew and were at that moment. Characters, landscapes, shooting, political slogans, jargon, curses, lyric flights, weapons, and love-making were only colors on the palette, notes of the scale; we knew all too well that what counted was the music and not the libretto. Though we were supposed to be concerned with content, there were never more dogged formalists than we; and never were lyric poets as effusive as those objective reporters we were supposed to be.

For us who began there, "neorealism" was this; and of its virtues and defects this book is a representative catalogue, born as it was from that green desire to make literature, a desire characteristic of the "school." Some people today recall "neorealism" chiefly as a contamination or constraint suffered by literature for extraliterary reasons, but this view shifts the terms of the question. Actually the extraliterary elements stood there so massive and so indisputable that they seemed a fact of nature; to us the whole problem was one of poetics; how to transform into a literary work that world which for us was *the* world.

"Neorealism" was not a school. (We must try to state things precisely.) It was a collection of voices, largely marginal, a multiple discovery of the various Italys, even —or particularly—the Italys previously unknown to literature. Without the variety of Italys unknown (or presumedly unknown) to one another, without the variety of dialects and jargon that could be kneaded and molded into the literary language, there would have been no "neorealism." But it was not provincial, in the sense of the regional *verismo* of the nineteenth century. Local characterization was intended to give the flavor of truth to a depiction in which the whole wide world was to be recognized: like the rural America of those 1930s writers whose direct or indirect disciples so many critics accused us of being. Therefore language, style, pace had so much importance for us, for this realism of ours which was to be as distant as possible from naturalism. We had drawn a line for ourselves, or rather a triangle—Verga, Vittorini, Pavese —from which to set out, each on the bases of his own local vocabulary and his own landscape. (I continue speaking in the plural, as if I were referring to an organized, conscious movement, now when I am explaining it was just the opposite. How easy it is, when you talk of literature, even in the midst of the most serious, factual discussion, to shift unaware to inventing stories. . . . For this reason discussions of literature irritate me more and more —the talk of others and my own as well.)

My landscape was something jealously mine (and this is where I could begin my preface: reducing to the minimum the "autobiography of a literary generation" lead, starting at once to speak of what concerns me directly, perhaps I can avoid being generic, approximate. . . .), a landscape that no one had ever really put on paper. (Except for the poet Montale—though he was from the other Ligurian Riviera—Montale, who I thought could be read as memory of our common landscape, in both his images and his vocabulary.) I came from the Riviera di Ponente; from the landscape of my city, San Remo, I polemically erased all the tourist shore—the sea front with its palm trees, casino, hotels, villas—as if I were ashamed of it. I began from the narrow alleys of the Old City, I climbed up the stream beds, I shunned the geometrical fields of carnations, I preferred the terraces of vineyards and olive groves with crumbling old dry walls, I ventured along the mule-tracks over the sedge-covered hills, up to where the woods begin, pines first, then chestnuts, and so I had gone from the sea—always visible from above, a stripe between two green flanks—to the tortuous valleys of the Ligurian Pre-Alps.

I had a landscape. But if I was to depict it, it had to become secondary to something else: to people, to stories. The Resistance represented the fusion of landscape with people. The novel I would never have been able to write otherwise is here. The daily scene of my whole life had become entirely extraordinary and adventurous: a single story unwound from the dark arches of the Old City up to the woods. It was the pursuit and the concealment of armed men. I succeeded in depicting even the villas, now that I had seen them requisitioned and transformed into guardhouses and prisons; even the fields of carnations, since they had become a no man's land, dangerous to cross, evoking a rattle of automatic fire in the air. It was from this possibility of setting human stories in landscapes that "neorealism" . . .

In this novel (I had better pick up the thread again; it is too early to start writing an apology for "neorealism"; even today analyzing the reasons for our break with it is more consonant with our mood), the marks of the literary period mingle with those of the author's youth. The exacerbation of the themes of violence and sex in the end appears ingenuous (today the reader's palate is accustomed to swallowing far more scorching fare) and forced (the fact that for the author these themes were exterior and temporary is proved by his later work).

The determination to insert ideological argument into the story can seem just as ingenuous and forced, especially with a story like this, founded on quite a different basis: a tone of immediate, objective depiction, both in language

and in images. To satisfy the necessity of the ideological
insertion, I used the expedient of concentrating all the
theoretical reflections in a single chapter whose tone is
detached from the others, Chapter Nine, the one containing reflections of Commissar Kim, almost like a preface
set in the middle of the novel. This expedient was criticized
by all my very first readers, who advised me to cut out the
whole chapter. I realized that the book's homogeneity suffered (at that time stylistic unity was one of the few certain aesthetic criteria; the juxtapositions of different styles
and languages that triumph today had not yet come back
into fashion), but I held out: the book had been born like
this, with this composite, illegitimate element.

The other big theme of future critical discussions, the
language-dialect theme, is present here in its ingenuous
phase: the dialect clotted into patches of color (whereas
in the narratives I was to write later I tried to absorb it all
into the language, like a vital but hidden plasma); uneven
writing, which at times is almost precious and at other
times flows as it comes, wholly given over to immediate
depiction; a documentary-like repertory (sayings, songs)
which almost arrives at folklore. . . . The problem of the
tenses of the verbs: since the simple past tense does not
exist in dialect, and to use the perfect would have been
monotonous, I decided to write the whole novel in the
present tense. . . .

And further (I continue the list of signs of age, my
own and general; a preface written today makes sense only
if it is critical), the way of describing the human character:
exaggerated and grotesque features, twisted grimaces, obscure visceral-collective dramas. Italian literary and figurative culture had missed the appointment with expression-
ism in the post–World War I period, but it had its great

moment after World War II. Perhaps the right name for that Italian season, instead of "neorealism," should be "neo-expressionism."

The distortions of the expressionistic lens are reflected in this book on the faces that had belonged to my beloved companions. I took pains to disguise them, to make them unrecognizable, "negative," because I found a poetic meaning only in "negativity." And at the same time I felt remorse toward reality, so much more variegated and warm and undefinable, toward the real people who I knew were humanly far richer and better, a remorse I was to carry with me for years. . . .

This was my first novel. What effect does it have on me, when I reread it now? (Now I have found the point: this remorse. This is where I should begin the preface.) The uneasiness this book caused me for so long has, in part, been attenuated; in part, it remains. It is the relationship with something far larger than myself, with emotions that involved all my contemporaries, and tragedies, and acts of heroism, of generosity, of genius, and dark dramas of conscience. The Resistance: where does this book stand in the "literature of the Resistance"? At the time I wrote it, creating a "literature of the Resistance" seemed an imperative; barely two months after the Liberation, Vittorini's *Uomini e no* had appeared in the bookshops' windows, containing our primordial dialect of death and happiness. Milan's urban guerrillas had had their novel at once, all rapid sorties over the city's concentric map; we who had been mountain partisans wanted our own novel, with our own different pace and different movements. . . .

Not that I was so culturally ignorant that I did not know history's influence on literature is indirect, slow, often contradictory. I knew well that many great historical events had occurred without inspiring a great novel, even during the "century of the novel" par excellence. I knew the great novel of the Risorgimento had never been written. We all knew, we were not that ingenuous; but I believe that whenever one has witnessed or participated in a historic period, he feels a special responsibility. . . .

In my case, this responsibility made me feel, finally, that the theme was too important and solemn for my powers. And then, to avoid being intimidated by the theme, I decide to tackle it not head-on but obliquely. Everything would be seen through the eyes of a child, in an atmosphere of urchins and tramps. I invented a story that would remain at the edge of the partisan war, its heroism and sacrifices, but at the same time would convey its color, its harsh flavor, its pace. . . .

This was my first novel. How can I define it now, re-examine it after so many years? (I must begin all over again. I had set off in the wrong direction: I was about to end up showing that this novel sprang from a clever evasion of "engagement," whereas on the contrary . . .) I can define it as an example of "engaged" literature in the most rich and full meaning of the word. Today, generally, when "engaged literature" is discussed, an erroneous idea is created, as if it were a literature employed to illustrate an already determined thesis, independently of any poetic expression. Instead, what was called "engagement," that kind of commitment, can crop up at every level; here it means, first of all, image and word, attitude, pace, style, contempt, defiance.

In the choice of the theme itself there is already an ostentation of almost provocatory boldness. Toward whom?

I would say I wanted to fight simultaneously on two fronts, challenging the Resistance's detractors and, at the same time, those high priests of a hagiographic and edulcorated Resistance.

First front: hardly more than a year after the Liberation, "right-minded respectability" was already on the upsurge again, exploiting every contingent aspect of that time —the confusion of postwar youth, the recrudescence of crime, the difficulty of establishing a new legality—to exclaim: "There, we said so all along; these Partisans, they're all like that; they needn't come telling us tales of the Resistance; we know perfectly well the sort of ideals. . . ."

This was the climate in which I wrote my book, which was meant to answer those right-minded, paradoxically: "Very well, I'll act as if you were right. I won't portray the finest partisans, but the worst ones possible. I'll focus my novel on a unit made up entirely of pretty devious characters. What does that change? Even those who flung themselves into the fight without any clear motivation were driven by an elementary impulse of human rescue, an impulse that made them a hundred thousand times better than you, that made them active forces of history such as you could never dream of being!" The sense of this argument, of this defiance is remote now; and even then, I must say, the book was read simply as a novel, not as an element in the discussion of a historic judgment. All the same, if you still feel a certain tingle of provocation, it comes from the controversy of that time.

From the double controversy. Even if the battle on the second front, the one inside "left-wing culture," also seems remote now. The attempt at "political direction" of literary activity was just beginning. The writer was being asked to create a "positive hero," to provide normative images, pedagogical standards of social behavior, of revolutionary militancy. This, as I said, was just beginning; and I must add that, then and later, such pressures did not have much effect or much support here in Italy. Nevertheless, the danger of the new literature's being assigned a celebratory, didactic function was in the air. When I wrote this book I had barely sensed it, but my hackles had already risen, my claws were bared against the menace of a new bombast. (We maintained our anticonformity intact then: an endowment difficult to preserve. But though it has known some occasional, partial eclipses, it still sustains us in this far more facile but no less dangerous period. . . .)

My reaction at that time could be expressed thus: "Ah, so you want the 'socialist hero,' eh? You want 'revolutionary romanticism,' do you? Well, I'll write you a partisan story in which nobody is a hero, nobody has any class consciousness. I'll give you the world of the *lingère*, the tramps, the Lumpenproletariat! [A new concept for me then; and it seemed a big discovery. I did not know that it had been and would continue to be the easiest terrain for fiction.] And this will be the most positive, the most revolutionary of works! What do we care about men who are heroic already, already socially conscious? It is the process toward those things that must be described! As long as there is one individual who has not gained that awareness, our duty is to concern ourselves with him, and only with him!"

This was how I reasoned, and with this polemical rage I flung myself into writing and I distorted the features and the character of people who had been my dearest companions, with whom for months and months I had shared a mess tin of chestnuts and the risk of death, for whose fate I had feared, whose nonchalance I had admired as they burned their bridges behind them, as I had admired their way of life free of egoisms; and I made them masks, contracted by constant grimaces, grotesque figures. I created dense chiaroscuro clouds—or what in my youthful naïvete I imagined might be chiaroscuro clouds—around their stories. . . . Only to feel afterward a remorse that was to dog me for years. . . .

I still have to start this preface once more, from the beginning. I have not yet got it right. From what I have said, it would seem that, writing this book, I had the whole thing quite clear in my mind: the reasons, arguments, the adversaries to combat, the poetic to sustain. . . . Instead, if all this was there, it was still in a confused, shapeless stage. Actually the book came forth as if by chance; I started writing without a precise plot in mind. I set out from that urchin character, from an element of direct observation of reality, a way of moving, of speaking, of establishing a rapport with grownups. To give this a fictional base, I invented the story of the sister, the pistol stolen from the Germans. Then the arrival among the partisans proved a difficult development; the leap from picaresque tale to collective epic threatened to spoil everything. I had to have an invention that would allow me to maintain the whole story on the same level, and I invented the detachment of Dritto.

As always, it was the story itself that imposed almost obligatory solutions. But in this plan, this pattern being formed as if on its own, I decanted my own still-fresh experience, a host of voices and faces (I distorted the faces, I tortured the people as any writer always does, so that reality became clay, instrument; and the writer knows this is the only way he can write, though he feels remorse all the same. . . .), a flood of arguments and reading interwoven with that experience.

Reading and experience of life are not two universes, but one. Every experience of life, in order to be interpreted, calls on certain readings and is fused with them. The fact that books are always born from other books is a truth, only apparently in contradiction with that other truth: that books are born from practical life and from relationships with human beings. We had just ended our partisan activity when we discovered (first in fragments published in magazines, then the whole book) a novel about the war in Spain that Hemingway had written six or seven years before: *For Whom the Bell Tolls*. It was the first book in which we recognized ourselves. This was where we began transforming into narratives themes and sentences that we had seen, felt, lived. The unit of Pablo and Pilar was our unit. (Today that is perhaps the book of Hemingway's I like least; in fact, even then it was the discovery of other books of his—especially the first stories —with the true lesson of his style, that made Hemingway our author.)

The literature we were interested in carried this sense of teeming humanity and mercilessness and nature. The Russians too, at the time of the Civil War—before Soviet literature became so Victorian and oleographic—we felt as our contemporaries, especially Babel, whose *Red Cavalry* we knew in an Italian translation even before the war, one of the exemplary books of our century's realism, born from the relationship between the intellectual and revolutionary violence.

This literature lies behind *Il sentiero dei nidi di ragno*. But in one's youth, every new book read is like a new eye opened, changing the sight of the other eyes or book-eyes one had before. And in the new idea of literature I was longing to create, all the literary universes that had enchanted me from childhood on lived again. . . . So, in setting myself to write something like Hemingway's *For Whom the Bell Tolls,* I also wanted to write something like Stevenson's *Treasure Island.*

Cesare Pavese caught on immediately, and from *Il sentiero* he guessed all my literary favorites. Pavese was the first to speak of a fairy-tale quality in my writing; and I, who had not realized it till then, was all too aware of it afterward, and attempted to confirm his definition. My story was beginning to be written down, and now it seems to me all contained in that beginning.

Perhaps, finally, your first book is the only one that matters. Perhaps a writer should write only that one. That is the one moment when you make the big leap; the opportunity to express yourself is offered that once, and you untie the knot within you then or never again. Perhaps poetry is possible only in one moment of a life, and for most people that moment is early youth. When it has passed, whether or not you have expressed yourself (and you will know only a hundred or a hundred and fifty years later; contemporaries cannot be good judges), after that the cards are on the table, you will come back only to imitate others or yourself, you will no longer succeed in saying a word that is true, irreplaceable. . . .

Interruption. Any discussion based on purely literary reasoning, if it is honest, ends in this blind alley, in this failure that writing always is. Luckily writing is not only a literary act; it is also something *else.* Once again, I feel obliged to correct the course this preface has taken.

This *else*, in my concerns of that time, was a definition of what partisan warfare had been. A friend and contemporary of mine, a doctor now, but then a student like me, spent whole evenings with me, arguing. For both of us the Resistance had been the fundamental experience: for him in a much more committed fashion, because he had been called on to assume grave responsibilities, and at just over twenty he had been Commissar of a partisan division, the one in which I had also taken part as a simple Garibaldino. It seemed to us then, a few months after the Liberation, that everyone was talking about the Resistance in the wrong way, a bombast was growing up, hiding its true essence, its basic character. It would be hard for me now to reconstruct our discussions; I remember only our constant argument against all mythicized images, our reduction of the partisan consciousness to a basic element that we had found in the simplest of our companions. It became the key to present and future history.

My friend was a cold, analytical debater, sarcastic toward everything that was not a fact. This book's only intellectual character, Commissar Kim, was meant to be a portrait of him; and something of our discussions of those days, our debate as to why those men without uniform or flag had fought, must have remained in my pages, in the dialogues between Kim and the brigade commander and in Kim's soliloquies.

These discussions were the background of the book, and, even before them, all my private reflections on violence, ever since I had found myself taking up arms. Before going off with the partisans, I had been a young bourgeois, who had always lived at home. My calm anti-Fascism was, most of all, opposition to the cult of warrior force; it was a matter of style, or sense of humor. Then suddenly coherence with my opinions led me into partisan violence, to measure myself by that other yardstick. It was a trauma, my first. . . .

And at the same time, there were reflections on moral judgment of people and on the historical meaning of the actions of each of us. For many of my contemporaries chance alone had determined the side for which they were to fight. Often roles were abruptly reversed: a die-hard Fascist became a partisan, or vice versa. Whatever side they were on, they shot and were shot at; only death gave their choice an irrevocable mark. (It was Pavese who could write: "Every victim resembles every survivor and asks him why," on the final page of *La casa in collina*, as he was trapped between his remorse at not having fought and his effort to be sincere about the reasons for his refusal.)

There: I have found how to lay out the preface. For months, after the end of the war, I tried to narrate the partisan experience in the first person, or with a protagonist who resembled me. I wrote some stories which were published; others I threw in the wastebasket. I moved awkwardly. I could never completely stifle the sentimental and moralistic vibrations. There was always a false note somewhere. To me, my personal history seemed humble, mean; I was full of complexes, inhibitions in the face of everything that meant the most to me.

As soon as I started writing stories in which I did not appear, all went smoothly: the language, rhythm, shape were precise, functional. The more I made the story objective, anonymous, the more it pleased me, and not only me. When I showed those stories to other members of the profession, people I had come to know in those early postwar days—Vittorini in Milan, Natalia Ginzburg and Pavese in Turin—they no longer voiced any objections. I began to realize that the more anonymous and objective the story was, the more it was mine.

Then the gift of "objective" writing seemed to me the most natural thing in the world; I could never have imagined I was to lose it so quickly. Every story moved with perfect confidence in a world I knew so well: this was *my* experience, my experience multiplied by the experience of the others. And historic significance, morality, sentiment were present precisely because I kept them hidden, implicit.

When I began planning a story about the character of a boy partisan I had known in our group, I did not think it would be longer than the others. Why did it turn into a novel? Because—I realized later—the identification between me and the protagonist had become something more complex. The relationship between the character of the boy Pin and the partisan war corresponded symbolically to the relationship with that war that I myself had come to have. Pin's inferiority, as a child in the face of the grownups' incomprehensible world, corresponds to my own, in the same situation, as a bourgeois. And Pin's audacity, due to his boasted underworld origins which make him feel the accomplice and virtually the superior of any "outlaw," corresponds to the "intellectual" way of mastering the situation, never being amazed, defending oneself from emotion. And so, thanks to these transpositions (which, mind you, I realized only a posteriori, a later help to explain to myself what I had written), the story from which my personal viewpoint had been banned became once again *my* story. . . .

My story was the story of an adolescence that lasted too long, for the young man who had used the war as an *alibi*, in both the original and figurative meaning of the word. In the space of a few years, the *alibi* had become a *here and now*. Too soon for me, or too late: dreams dreamed too long, and I was unprepared for living them. First, the reversal of the alien war, the transformation into heroes and chiefs of yesterday's obscure rebels. Now, in peacetime, the fervor of new energies that animated all relationships, invaded all instruments of public life, and suddenly also the remote castle of literature opened like a nearby, friendly refuge, ready to welcome the provincial youth with fanfares and banners. And an amorous charge electrified the air, brightened the eyes of the girls that war and peace had restored to us and made closer, now truly coeval, companions, in an understanding that was the new gift of those first months of peace, filling the warm evenings of resuscitated Italy with dialogue and laughter.

Among all these beckoning possibilities, I was unable to be what I had dreamed before the hour of the test: I had been the last of the partisans; I was an uncertain and unsatisfied and unskilled lover; literature did not offer itself as a casual, detached skill but was more like a road on which I was unable to start out. Filled with youthful desire and tension, I was denied the spontaneous grace of youth. The sudden ripening of the times only accentuated my own unripeness.

So the symbolic protagonist of my book was an image of regression: a child. To Pin's childish, jealous gaze, weapons and women were again distant and incomprehensible. What my philosophy exalted, my poetics transfigured in enemy apparitions, my excess of love dyed with infernal desperation.

As I wrote, my stylistic requirement was to remain below events. The Italian speech I liked was that of someone who "doesn't speak Italian at home." I tried to write as a hypothetical, autodidact me would have written.

Il sentiero dei nidi di ragno was born from this sense of absolute lack of property, half suffered to the point of torment, half imagined and vaunted. If I find any value in the book today it lies there: in the image of a still-obscure vital power where the indigence of the "too young" man is soldered with the indigence of the outcast and the rejected.

When I say that we then made literature out of our condition of poverty, I am not speaking so much of an ideological program as of something deeper in each of us.

Nowadays, when writing is a regular profession, when the novel is a "product" with its "market," its "demand" and its "supply," with its advertising campaigns, its successes, and its routine, now that Italian novels are all "of a good average level" and are among the superfluous goods of a too quickly satisfied society, it is hard to recall the spirit in which we tried to initiate a kind of fiction that still had to be built entirely with our own hands.

I continue to use the plural, but I have already explained that I am speaking of something dispersed, not agreed upon, something that emerged from the scattered corners of the provinces, without explicit common reasons, unless they were partial and temporary. More than anything else it was, you could say, a widespread potential, something in the air. And soon extinct.

By the 1950s the picture had changed, starting with the masters: Pavese dead, Vittorini sealed off in a silence of opposition, Alberto Moravia in a different context, tak-

ing on a different meaning (no longer existential but
naturalistic); and the Italian novel assumed its elegiac-
moderate sociological course. We all finally dug ourselves
niches, more or less comfortable (or found our own ave-
nues of escape).

But there were some who continued along the path
of that first, fragmentary epic. For the most part, they were
the more isolated, the outsiders, who retained that strength.
And it was the most solitary of all who succeeded in creating the novel we had all dreamed of, when none of us expected it any longer. Beppe Fenoglio succeeded in writing
it, in *Il partigiano Johnny*, but not in finishing it. He died
before it was published, in his forties.

This was my first novel, almost my first piece of writing.
What can I say about it today? I will say this: it would
always be better not to have written one's first book.

As long as your first book remains unwritten, you
possess that freedom which you can use only once in a
lifetime. Your first book already defines you, while you are
really far from being defined. And this definition is something you may then carry with you for the rest of your
life, trying to confirm it or extend or correct or deny it; but
you can never eliminate it.

Moreover: for those who began writing young, after
one of those experiences with "so many things to say" (the
war, in this case and in many others), the first book immediately becomes a partition between you and experience; it severs the ties that bind you to events; it burns up
the treasure of memory—what would have become a treasure if you had had the patience to preserve it, if you had
not been in such a hurry to spend it, to squander it, to
impose an arbitrary hierarchy on the images you had

stored up, separating the favorites, the presumed containers of poetic emotion, from those others that seemed to concern you too much or too little for you to be able to portray them—setting up, in other words, arrogantly, another transfigured memory in the place of the general memory with its vague outlines, its infinite possibilities of rediscovery. . . . Your memory will never recover from this violence you have done it in writing: the favored images will be consumed by their premature promotion to literary themes, while the images you wanted to keep in reserve, perhaps with the secret intention of using them in future works, will wither, because they are cut off from the natural wholeness of vital, flowing memory. The literary projection, where all is solid and fixed for good, has now occupied the field, has faded and crushed the vegetation of memories where the life of the tree and that of the blade of grass are reciprocally conditioned. Memory—or rather experience, which is memory plus the wound it has left in you, plus the change it has worked in you that has made you different—experience, first nourishment also of literary work (but not only of that), true wealth for the writer (but not only for him), now, as soon as it has given shape to a literary work, declines, is destroyed. The writer finds himself once again the poorest of men.

And so I look back, to that season which appeared to me crammed with images and meanings: the partisan war, the months that were worth years and from which for a lifetime one should have been able to extract faces and warnings and landscapes and thoughts and episodes and words and emotions. And everything is distant and misty, and the written pages are there, in their shameless confidence which I well know is fraudulent, the written pages already arguing against a moment that was still a present, massive fact, which seemed stable, given, once and for all, *experience*—and they are no use to me. I would need all the rest, the very things that are not there. A written book will never console me for what I destroyed in writing it: that experience which, if cherished through the years of a lifetime, would perhaps have served me to write the last book, though it sufficed only for me to write the first.

June 1964

ITALO CALVINO
Translated from the Italian by William Weaver

CHAPTER ONE

THE OLD towns on the Ligurian coast grew up in times when those parts were infested by Moorish pirates; built to resist siege, they are as close and dense as pine-cones; their deep narrow alleys, called *carrugi*, are spanned by arches propping the tops of the houses, with dark vaulted arcades and flights of cobbled steps running far below.

Life in one of these old towns, towards the end of 1944, seems back in the times of the Moorish sieges; after curfew only armed patrols circulate in the alleys; a feeble light flickers from the street lanterns; the walls are stacked with sandbags; and when ships appear out at sea the population coops itself up underground.

To reach the depths of the alleys the sun's rays must go straight down, grazing the cold walls and falling over windows scattered haphazard here and there, over tufts of basil and marjoram planted in cooking pots on the sills, and under-clothes hung out to dry.

In Long Alley, the *carrugio* with the worst reputation in the town, the first to put his nose out is Pin, the cobbler's apprentice. He calls, begins a song, and a chorus of shouts and insults pours from every window. The alley begins another day.

"Pin! At it already, making our lives a misery! Sing us one of your songs, Pin! Pin, you little wretch, what's he doing to you? Pin, you little monkey-face! If only your throat would dry in your guts! You and that chicken-thief of a master of yours! You and that mattress of a sister of yours!"

But by now Pin is standing in the middle of the alley, with his hands in the pockets of a jacket that's too big for him, looking up at them one by one with an unsmiling face: "Hey, Celestino, you'd better keep quiet, you with that fine

1

new suit of yours. They haven't found out yet who stole that stuff from the quays, have they? Hallo, Carolina, you were lucky that time. Yes. Lucky your husband didn't look under the bed that time."

Pin has the hoarse voice of a much older boy; he shouts out his jeers in deep, serious tones, then suddenly breaks into a laugh with a note as high and sharp as a whistle, while red and black freckles cluster up round his eyes like a swarm of wasps.

Insulting Pin is always risky; he knows all the inside gossip of the alley and one can never tell what he'll come out with. From morning till night he's out there under the windows singing and shouting at the top of his voice, while in Pietromagro's shop the pile of unmended shoes almost buries the cobbler's bench and spills out into the street.

"Pin, you little monkey! You little horror!" a woman shouts at him. "Resole those slippers for me instead of standing there making a nuisance of yourself all day! They've been in that pile a month. I'll have something to say to your master when they let him out!"

Pietromagro spends half his life in prison, for he was born without luck, and whenever there's a theft in the neighbourhood he's always the one to be eventually put inside. He gets out to find that great pile of unmended shoes in an empty shop. Then he sits down at his cobbler's bench, takes up a shoe, turns it over once or twice, throws it back into the heap, and finally puts his hairy face into his bony hands and begins swearing. When Pin, knowing nothing, comes in whistling, he is suddenly faced by Pietromagro, with a face covered in short black hair like dog's fur, eyes ringed with yellow round the pupils, and hand upraised. Pin screams, but Pietromagro has already caught him and does not let go. When Pietromagro is tired of hitting Pin he leaves him in the shop and makes for the tavern. No one sees any more of him that day.

On alternate evenings Pin's sister is visited by a German

sailor. Every time the man makes his way up the alley, Pin waits for him to ask for a cigarette. The sailor was generous at first and even gave him three or four at a time. It's easy for Pin to make fun of the German, who can't understand what he says and looks at him from a shapeless congealed-looking face, shaven to the temples. Then, when the sailor's back is turned, Pin can shout insults after him, certain he won't turn round. Seen from behind the sailor looks ridiculous, with those two black ribbons hanging down from his little cap over his short tunic to his bare-looking bottom; a fleshy bottom, like a woman's, with a big German pistol dangling over it.

"Little pimp . . . little pimp . . ." people call down from the windows at Pin, not too loudly though, as one never knows with those Germans.

"Cuckolds . . . cuckolds . . ." Pin shouts back, copying their voices, and gulping down cigarette smoke that feels sharp and rough against his tender throat, but which has to be gulped down, who knows why, till his eyes water and he breaks into a violent fit of coughing. Then, with the cigarette still in his mouth, off he goes to the tavern and calls out: "By God, I'll tell anyone who stands me a glass of wine something he'd like to hear."

In the tavern are the same men who have been there all day long for years, sitting with their elbows on the tables and their chins in their fists, gazing at the flies on the sticky paper and the purple stains in the bottom of their glasses.

"What's up?" says Michel the Frenchy. "Has your sister reduced her prices?"

The others laugh and pound their fists on the zinc table-tops: "You've had the reply you deserve this time, Pin!"

Pin stands there looking them up and down through the spiky fringe of hair covering his forehead.

"God, just as I thought. Look at him, he thinks of nothing but my sister. Never stops thinking of her, I tell you. He's in love. In love with my sister, God help him. . . ."

The others roar with laughter and clap him on the back and pour him out a glass. Pin does not like wine; it feels harsh against his throat and wrinkles his skin up and makes him long to laugh and shout and stir up trouble. Yet he drinks it, swallowing down each glassful in one gulp, as he swallows cigarette smoke, or as at night he watches with shivers of disgust his sister lying with some man on her bed, a sight like the feel of a rough hand moving over his skin, harsh like all sensations men enjoy; smoke, wine, women.

"Sing, Pin," they say. And Pin begins singing, seriously, tensely, in that hoarse childish voice of his. He sings a song called "The Four Seasons":

> *When I think of the future*
> *And the liberty I've lost*
> *I'd like to kiss her and then die*
> *While she sleeps . . . and never knows.*

The men sit listening in silence, with their eyes lowered, as if to a hymn. All of them have been to prison; no-one is a real man to them unless he has. And the old jail-birds' song is full of the melancholy which seeps into the bones in prison, at night, when the warders pass hitting the grills with a crowbar, and gradually the quarrels and curses die down, and all that can still be heard is a voice singing this song which Pin is singing now, and which no one shouts for him to stop.

> *At night I love to hear*
> *The sentry's call,*
> *I love to watch the passing moon*
> *Light up my cell.*

Pin has never been in a real prison yet; once when they tried to take him off to a reformatory he escaped. Every now and again he is picked up by the municipal guards for some escapade among the stalls in the fruit-market, but he always sends the guards nearly crazy with his screams and sobs, until finally they let him go. He has been shut up in their guard-room once or twice, though, and knows what prison feels like; that's why he is singing this song so well, with real emotion.

Pin knows a lot of old songs which have been taught him by the men of the tavern, songs about violence and bloodshed such as "Torna Cascrio" or the one about a soldier called Peppino who killed his lieutenant. Then, when they are all feeling sad and gazing into the purple depths of their glasses, Pin suddenly twirls round the smoky room and begins singing at the top of his voice:

> *And I touched her hair —*
> *And she said not there . . .*

Then the men begin pounding on the tables and shouting "hiuú," and clapping time, while the servant-girl tries to save the glasses. And the women in the tavern, old drunks with red faces like the one called the Bersagliera, sway to and fro as if to the rhythm of a dance. And Pin, the blood running in his head and gritting his teeth with the effort, seems to be throwing his very soul into the song as he shouts at the top of his voice:

> *And I touched her ear —*
> *And she said, my dear . . .*

And all of them, clapping time to the swaying of the old Bersagliera, break into the chorus: *"Lovey if you like me . . ."*

That day the German sailor had come up the alley in a bad temper. Hamburg, his native town, was being ravaged by bombs every night, and every day he was waiting for news of his wife and children. He had a warm nature, this German had, a southern nature in the body of a man from the North Sea. He had filled his own home with children, and now, when the war had moved him far away, tried to cool off his oppressive heat by attaching himself to prostitutes in the occupied countries.

"No cigarettes," he had said to Pin who was coming towards him to say *guten Tag*. Pin began to frown.

"Well, lad, you'll be feeling a bit nostalgic to-day, eh?" he said.

Now it was the German's turn to frown at Pin; he could not understand.

"Are you on your way to visit my sister, by any chance?" said Pin carelessly.

The German then said: "Sister not home?"

"What, don't you know?" Pin's expression was so sly he might have been brought up by priests. "Don't you know they've taken her off to hospital? Poor thing! It's bad, that disease, but curable now, if taken in time. Of course she'd had it on her for a bit . . . think of her in hospital, poor thing!"

The German's face looked like curdled milk. "Hos-pit-al? Di-sea-se?" he stuttered and sweated. Then in a window just above the ground floor appeared the head and shoulders of a young woman with a horse face and frizzy black hair.

"Don't you take any notice of him, Frick, don't take any notice of the little squirt," she screamed. "I'll make you pay for this, monkey-face, you nearly ruined me! Come on up, Frick, don't take any notice of him, he was only joking, devil take him!"

Pin put his tongue out at her. "I got you into a cold sweat, *Kamarad*," he said to the German, as he slipped away down a side-alley.

Sometimes, after a malicious joke of that kind, Pin finds himself with a bitter taste in his mouth, and wanders round the alleys alone, with everyone cursing him and pushing him aside. Then he longs to go off with a band of young companions to whom he could show the place where spiders make their nests, or with whom he could have battles among the bamboos in the river-bed. But Pin is not liked by boys of his own age; he is the friend of grown-ups, Pin is, he can say things to grown-ups that make them laugh or get angry, while other boys can't even understand what grown-ups say to each other. Pin sometimes feels a longing to ask boys of his own age to let him play with them, to show him the way into the underground passage that goes right under the Market Square. But the other boys take no notice of him; sometimes they even set on him, for Pin has tiny thin arms and is the weakest of them all. Now and again they go and ask Pin to explain what happens between men and women; but he begins making fun of them in a loud voice down the alley, and the mothers call their sons inside: "Costanzo! Giacomino! How often have I told you not to go about with that nasty little boy!"

The mothers are right. All Pin talks about is men and women in bed, or men murdered or put in prison, stories picked up from grown-ups, fables they tell among themselves — the other little boys think — and which would be nice to stop and listen to if only Pin did not intersperse them with jeers and remarks they cannot understand.

So Pin is forced to take refuge again in the world of grown-ups, of men who turn their backs on him and are as incomprehensible and far-removed from him as they are from the other little boys, but who are easier to make fun of, with their yearning for women and their terror of the police, till they tire of him and begin to curse him.

Now Pin will go back into the smoky violet air of the tavern, and mouth obscenities and insults to the men there until he has whipped them up into a frenzy and they begin attacking each other; then he'll sing sentimental songs with all his might till he makes them cry and is crying himself, then invent new jokes and grimaces till he's hysterical with laughter, all to disperse the cloud of loneliness which settles round his heart on evenings like this.

But the men in the tavern now all have their backs turned, forming an impenetrable wall; there in the middle of them is a newcomer, a thin serious-looking man. As Pin comes in the men frown at him, then at the unknown man, and say something. Pin feels that the atmosphere is different; all the more reason to go up to the group with his hands in his pockets and say: "God, you ought to have seen that German's face!"

The men don't make their usual joking replies, but turn slowly round one by one. Frenchy Michel first frowns at him as if he's never seen him before, then says slowly: "You're a filthy little pimp."

The freckles cloud up like wasps round Pin's eyes, then he says calmly, though his eyes are slits: "Perhaps you'll tell me why?"

Giraffe twists his neck slightly round towards him and says: "Off you go, we don't want to see anyone who deals with Germans."

"With your contacts, you and your sister," says Gian the driver, "you'll end up as important Fascists."

Pin tries to put on the expression he uses when they make fun of him.

"Perhaps you'll tell me what all this is about," he says, "I've never had anything to do with the Fascio, not even the Balilla, and my sister goes with whoever she feels inclined to and does no one any harm."

Michel scratches his face a little. "The day everything changes — you know what I mean — the day everything changes we'll send your sister round town with her head as shaved and bare as a plucked chicken . . . And for you . . . for you we'll think up something you haven't even dreamt of."

Pin does his best to look unconcerned, but is obviously suffering inwardly, and is biting his lips. "On the day when you get a bit brighter," he says, "I'll explain how things are. First, that I and my sister each go our own way, and as for pimping you can go and do it for her yourself if you feel like it. Second, that my sister doesn't go with Germans because she particularly likes them, but because she's as international as the Red Cross; and the same way she goes with Germans now she'll go later with English, Negroes and anyone else who happens to turn up" . . . (all these are things Pin has learnt from listening to grown-ups, probably the very same ones he's talking to now. Why should he have to explain them?) "Third, the only dealings I've had with that German is getting cigarettes out of him, in return for which I've played tricks on him like the one I did to-day, which I won't tell you about as you've put me in a bad temper."

But the attempt to change the subject does not succeed. Gian the driver says: "Tricks! I've been in Croatia and there a bloody German only had to go looking round a village for women, and he was never seen again, nor was his corpse."

Michel says: "One day or the other he'll be found dead in a ditch, your German will."

The unknown man, who has been silent all this time without smiling or showing any signs of approval, now pulls Michel by the sleeve a little: "That's the sort of thing you mustn't say. Remember what I told you."

The others are now looking at Pin in silence. What can they want of him?

"Say," exclaims Michel, "have you seen what a pistol that sailor has?"

"Yes, a hell of a big pistol," replies Pin.

"Well," says Michel, "you must steal that pistol from him."

"How can I do that?" exclaims Pin.

"Try."

"But how? He always wears it clamped to his bottom. You go and steal it."

"Well, let's see . . . Doesn't he take his trousers off at a certain moment? Then he must take his pistol off too, surely. Go and steal it. Try."

"I will if I feel like it."

"Listen," says Giraffe, "we aren't joking here. If you want to be one of us you know what you must do. Otherwise . . ."

"Otherwise . . ."

"Otherwise . . . D'you know what a G.A.P.[1] is?"

The unknown man gives Giraffe a nudge and shakes his head; he does not seem to like the way the others are behaving.

New words to Pin always have a halo of mystery, a hint of something dark and forbidden. A *Gap?* What could a *Gap* be?

"Yes, of course I know what it is," he says.

"What is it?" asks Giraffe.

"It's where you all blasted well belong, you and your family."

But the men aren't listening to him. The unknown man has signed to them to bring their heads close and is whispering to them and seems to be rebuking them for something, and they are making signs of agreement.

Pin is out of all this. He can creep away without saying a word; perhaps it's best, he thinks, not to mention that business of the pistol any more, it probably wasn't important, and they may have forgotten all about it.

But Pin has just reached the door when Michel raises his head and says: "Pin, then we're agreed about that."

Pin would like to begin acting the fool again, but suddenly he feels a child surrounded by grown-ups, and stands there with his hand on the jamb of the door.

"If not don't put your face in here again," says Michel.

Now Pin is outside, in the alley. Dusk is falling and lights are going on in the windows. Far away, down by the river, frogs are beginning to croak; at this time of the year boys spend their evenings hanging over pools, trying to catch them. If they do, the frogs feel slimy and slithery in their hands, smooth and naked as women.

A little boy in glasses and long trousers passes by: Battistino.

---

[1] *Gruppo Azione Patrioti.* The smallest unit of the Italian partisan organisation, usually in towns.

"Battistino, d'you know what a *Gap* is?"

Battistino blinks with curiosity. "No, tell me. What is it?"

Pin breaks out into a peal of laughter. "Just go and ask your mother what a *Gap* is. Say to her, 'Mummy, will you give me a *Gap*?' Say that. She'll explain, you just see!"

Battistino goes off, looking vexed.

Pin wanders up the alley, which is almost dark now, and feels alone and lost amid all this talk of bloodshed and naked bodies which makes up men's lives.

CHAPTER TWO

HIS SISTER's room, from where Pin is looking at it, seems filled with mist; he can see a vertical strip crowded with objects and surrounded by muzzy shadows, with everything changing dimensions according to whether he puts his eye nearer or farther from the slit. It's like looking through a woman's stocking; the smell is the same too: his sister's smell emanating from the other side of the wooden partition and coming perhaps from those rumpled clothes and that bed which is never properly made, the sheets just flung back without ever being aired.

Pin's sister has always been careless about household matters ever since she was a child; when Pin was a baby and used to cry loudly in her arms, his head full of sores, she would leave him on a ledge of the wash-house and go off to skip with urchins around the chalk squares marked on the pavements. Every now and again their father's ship would return; all Pin could remember of him was being swung in the air in his big, bare arms, strong arms marked with black veins. But after their mother's death his visits became rarer and rarer, until he was never seen again; people said he had another family in a city beyond the sea.

Pin now lives in a cubby-hole of a room, a sort of kennel beyond a wooden partition, with a high narrow slit of a window, cut sideways through the thick wall of the old house. Beyond it is his sister's room, from which the light comes in streaks through the cracks in the partition, cracks which make Pin's eyes squint with the effort to see what's going on in the rest of the room. Pin has spent hours and hours at those cracks ever since he was a baby, and he's trained his eyes to be like needle points; he knows everything that happens inside there, though the reasons for it all elude him. When, in the end, he curls up in his little bunk with his arms round his chest, the shadows of the tiny room transform themselves into strange dreams, of bodies chasing each other, hitting and embracing, till something big and hot and unknown happens which paralyses Pin and yet caresses and warms him too; it seems the explanation of everything, like the faint distant memory of some forgotten happiness.

The German is now wandering round the room in his vest, his arms pink and meaty as thighs; every now and again he comes right up to the crack in the partition; at one moment Pin can also see his sister's legs, twirling in the air, then plunging under the sheets. Now Pin has to twist round to see where the German is putting down the belt with the pistol on it; there it is, hung on the back of a chair; Pin wishes he had an arm as narrow as the slit so that he could pass it through, reach the weapon and pull it towards him. Now the German is naked except for his vest; he's laughing; he always laughs when he's naked because he has a shy nature, deep down, like a girl's. He jumps into bed and puts out the light. Pin knows that a little time will go by in darkness and silence before the bed begins to creak.

Now is the moment. Pin must enter the room with bare feet, on all fours, and pull the belt down from the chair without making any noise; all this is just not a game to laugh and joke about afterwards; no, it is connected with something secret and mysterious said by the men in the tavern with an opaque look in the whites of their eyes. Yes, Pin would like always to be friends with grown-ups, for them always to joke with him and to take him into their confidence. Pin loves grown ups, he loves scoring off them — those strong stupid grown-ups all of whose secrets he knows. He even loves the German. And now he is doing something irreparable; perhaps he'll never be able to joke with the German again, after this; and things will be different with the men in the tavern, too; they'll have a link with him beyond laughter and obscenities, and will always look at him with those mysterious frowns and ask him strange things in low voices. Pin would like to stretch himself out on his little bed and lie there thinking with his eyes open, listening to the German and his sister on the other side of the partition, lie there imagining himself being accepted by bands of boys as their leader because he knows so much more than they do, and them all going out against the grown-ups together and beating them up and doing such wonderful things that the grown-ups are forced to admire him too and ask him to be their leader, loving him and stroking his head at the same time. But now, instead of that, he has to move about at night with the grown-ups hating him, and steal a pistol from a German, things not done by other boys, who play with tin pistols and wooden swords. What would they say if Pin went among them next day, and gradually revealed to them a real pistol, all shiny and menacing and looking as if it were about to go off on its own? Perhaps they would be frightened, and Pin would also be frightened of keeping such a thing under his jacket; all he needs, he thinks, to terrify the grown-ups so much that they fall down fainting and asking for mercy, is one of those toy pistols that fire a strip of red caps.

Instead of which Pin is now crawling on all fours into his sister's room, bare-foot, with his head already beyond the curtain, into that smell of male and female which goes straight to the nostrils. He can see the shadows of the furniture in the room, the bed, the chair, the oblong bidet on its triangular stand. There; now that dialogue of groans is beginning from the bed, and he can creep in on all fours, taking care to go very slowly. Perhaps, though, Pin would be pleased if the floor creaked, the German heard and suddenly put on the light, and he had to run out of the house on bare feet with his sister shouting behind him: "Little swine!"; pleased, perhaps, if the whole neighbourhood heard too and he could tell the story to Driver and Frenchy, with so many details that they would believe him and say: "All right. It went badly. Don't let's talk about it any more."

The floor does in fact creak, but so many other things are creaking at that moment that the German does not hear. Pin is now touching the belt, and it turns out to be quite solid, not magical, and it slips down from the back of the chair almost frighteningly easy, without even banging on the floor. Now "it" has happened; the fear he had only imagined before has become real fear. The belt must now be hurriedly wrapped round the holster, and all of it pushed under his vest without getting entangled in his arms and legs; the next thing to do is go back on his tracks on all fours, very slowly and without ever taking his tongue from between his teeth; if he took that tongue away perhaps something awful would happen.

Once out of the room he realises that he can't now go back to his little bed and hide the pistol under the mattress, as he does with apples stolen from the fruit market. In a short time the German will be getting up and looking for his pistol and turning the whole place upside down.

Pin goes out into the alley; the pistol is not worrying him very much at the moment; hidden like that in his clothes it is an object like any other and he can forget he has it; Pin rather regrets his own indifference, and would like to feel at least a shiver to remind him of it. A real pistol. A real pistol. Pin tries to excite himself with the thought. Someone who has a real pistol can do anything, he's like a grown-up. He can threaten to kill men and women and do whatever he likes with them.

Pin now thinks he will grasp the pistol and walk round with it always pointed at people; no one will be able to take it away from him and everyone will be afraid of him. But the pistol, wrapped in its belt, is still under his vest, and he cannot make up his mind to touch it; in a way he almost hopes that when he looks for it it will have vanished, melted away from the heat of his body.

The place to look at the pistol is a hidden flight of steps under an arch where children go to play hide-and-seek, lit only by a glimmer of light from a broken lantern. Pin unrolls the belt, opens the holster, and with a gesture as if he were taking a cat by the neck pulls out the pistol. It is really very big and threatening; if Pin had the courage to play with it he would pretend it was a cannon. But he handles it as if it were a bomb. The safety-catch, where can the safety-catch be?

Finally he decides to grasp it by the butt, though he's careful not to put his finger near the trigger; he holds it tightly; even like this he can imagine using it properly and pointing it against anyone he wants. Pin first points it at the gutter-pipe, right up against the metal, then at a finger, making a fierce face, drawing back his head and hissing: "Your money or your life"; then he finds an old shoe and points it against that, first the heel, then the inside; then he pushes the barrel down into the toe. What fun! A shoe, such an ordinary object, particularly for a cobbler's apprentice like him, and a pistol, such a mysterious, almost unreal thing; by putting them up against each other he can do wonders, make them tell marvellous tales.

But then suddenly Pin cannot resist the temptation any more and points the pistol against his temple; it makes his head swim. On it moves, until it touches the skin and he can feel the coldness of the steel. Suppose he put his finger on the trigger now? No, it's better to press the mouth of the barrel against his temple until it hurts, and feel the circle of steel with its empty centre where the bullets come from. Perhaps if he suddenly pulls the gun away from his temple, the suction of the air will make a shot go off; no, it doesn't go off. Now he can put the barrel into his mouth and feel its taste against his tongue. Then, the most frightening of all, put it up to his eyes and look right into it, down the dark barrel which seems deep as a well. Once Pin saw a boy who had shot himself in the eye with a sporting-gun being taken off to hospital; his face was half-covered by a great splodge of blood, and the other half with little black spots from the gunpowder.

Pin has now played with a real pistol. He has played with it enough, and can give it to the men who asked for it, he is now longing to give it to them, in fact. When he has not got it any more it will be the same as if he'd never stolen it, and the German can be as furious as he likes and Pin can laugh at him behind his back again.

His first impulse is to rush into the tavern and call out: "I've got it! I've got it!" amid general enthusiasm and exclamations of surprise. Then it occurs to him that it would be cleverer to say: "Guess what I've brought!" and keep them waiting a little before telling them. But they would be sure to think of the pistol at once, so he had better mention it at first and then go on to give them a dozen different versions of what happened, hinting that things went badly, until when they are on tenterhooks and have lost the drift, he'd put the pistol on the table and say: "Look what I've found in my pocket," and watch the expressions on their faces.

Pin enters the tavern silently, on tiptoe; the men are still talking round a table, their elbows looking as if they had taken root. Only the unknown man is no longer there; his chair is empty. Pin is now standing behind them and they have not noticed him; he waits for them to catch sight of him suddenly and start up with questioning looks. But no one turns. Pin moves a chair. Giraffe twists his neck round and frowns at him, then goes on talking in a low voice.

"Hey, men," exclaims Pin.

They give him a glance.

"Uglyface," says Giraffe, in a friendly way.

No one says anything else.

"Well . . ." says Pin.

"Well . . ." says Gian the driver. "What's new?"

Pin is beginning to feel rather deflated.

"Well . . ." says Michel the Frenchy. "Feeling low? Sing us a song, Pin."

They're pretending not to be interested, thinks Pin, but really they're longing to know what I've done.

"Don't you worry about that," exclaims Giraffe. "You worry about getting hold of that German's pistol, as we'd agreed."

Pin's ears go up. Now he'll say: "Just guess . . ."

"Make sure you don't lose sight of it, once you've set eyes on it."

This is not what Pin expected. Why do they care so little about it now? He begins to wish he had not taken the pistol, and feels like going back to the German and putting it back where it was.

"For a pistol," says Michel. "It's not worth risking much. Anyway it's an old model; heavy, it sticks."

"Meanwhile," says Giraffe, "we must show the committee we're doing something, that's the important thing." And they continue their discussion in low voices.

Pin cannot hear what they are saying. Now he's sure he won't give them the pistol; he has tears in his eyes and can feel his gums drawn with rage. Grown-ups are an untrustworthy treacherous lot, they don't take their games in the serious wholehearted way children do, and their own games are so complicated and involved that it's difficult to discover what the real one is. Before it seemed that they were playing a game with the unknown man against the German, now they are playing one on their own against the unknown man; what they say can never be trusted.

"Well, sing us something, then, Pin," they say now, as if nothing had happened, as if there had never been that definite pact between them, a pact consecrated by that mysterious word: *Gap*.

"*Alé*," says Pin, pale, his lips trembling. He knows he cannot sing now. He feels like bursting into tears; instead of which he breaks into a shriek high enough to break the eardrums, ending in a string of curses: "Bastards! Sons of filthy stinking cows of whores!"

The others stare at him, wondering what is wrong with him, but Pin has already rushed out of the tavern.

Outside, his first impulse is to look for that man, the one they call "Committee", and give him the pistol; he's the only one for whom Pin feels any respect now, though he had been so quiet and serious he had made Pin distrustful before. But now Pin feels that he is the only person who can understand him and admire what he has done; perhaps "Committee" would take Pin off to fight the Germans with him, just the two of them, armed with that pistol, firing from street corners. But who knew where Committee had gone to now? Pin cannot ask around after him, as no one had ever seen him before.

So Pin decides that he will keep the pistol himself and not give it to anyone or tell anyone that he has it. He'll just hint that he controls a terrible power, and everyone will obey him. Whoever owns a real pistol must be able to play wonderful games, games which no other boy has ever played. But Pin is a boy who does not know how to play games, and cannot take part in the games either of children or grown-ups. So he will go off now, away from everyone, and play with his pistol all on his own, games that no one else knows and no one else can ever learn.

It is dark now. Pin turns out of the huddle of old houses into paths running between vegetable patches and rubbish-pits. The wire-netting around the crops throws a network of grey shadows over the moonlit ground. The hens are now sleeping in rows on their perches in the coops, and the frogs are out of the water and chorusing away along the bed of the whole torrent, from source to mouth. What would happen if he shot at a frog? There'd be nothing left, perhaps, but green slime squashed on the stones.

Pin wanders along the paths which wind along the side of the torrent, stony parts which no one cultivates. Here there are paths which he alone knows and which the other boys would love to be told about. There is a place where spiders make their nests. Only Pin knows it. It's the only one in the whole valley, perhaps in the whole area. No other boy except Pin has ever heard of spiders that make nests.

Perhaps one day Pin will find a friend, a real friend, who understands him and whom he can understand, and then to him, and only to him, will he show the place where the spiders have their lairs. It's on a stony little path which winds down to the torrent between earthy grassy slopes. There, in the grass, the spiders make their nests, in tunnels lined with dry grass. But the wonderful thing is that the nests have tiny doors, also made of dried grass, tiny round doors which can open and shut.

When Pin has played some particularly cruel joke and has laughed so much that a heavy sadness has finally filled his chest, he wanders all alone along the paths in the little valley, looking for the place where the spiders make their nests. With a long stick he can probe right into the nests and skewer the spider, a small black spider with little grey markings on it, like those on the summer dresses of old village women.

It amuses Pin to break the doors of the nests down and skewer the spiders on sticks, and to catch grasshoppers and gaze close into their little horse-like faces, then cut them up into pieces and make strange designs with their legs on a smooth stone.

Pin is cruel to animals; to him they are as monstrous and incomprehensible as grown-ups; it must be horrible to be an insect, to be green, and always to be frightened that a human being like him might come along, with a huge face full of red and black freckles and fingers that can pull grasshoppers to bits.

Pin is now all alone among the spiders' nests, and around him is night, infinite as the chorus of the frogs. He is alone but he has the pistol with him; now he puts on the belt with its holster to dangle over his bottom like the German; only the German was fat and the belt hangs down on Pin like the bandoliers worn by warriors in the films. Now he can pull the pistol out with a grand gesture as if he were drawing a sword, and shout: "To the assault, my men!" as boys do when they play at pirates. But he cannot understand what pleasure those silly fools get in doing that; Pin, after jumping around on the grass for a time, waving the pistol and aiming it at the olive-trees, is already bored and does not know what to do with the gun next.

At that moment the spiders underground are gnawing away at flies or coupling together, males and females, giving out little threads of slime; they are as filthy as men are, Pin thinks, and he pushes the barrel of the pistol into the opening of a nest, longing to kill them. What would happen if a shot went off? The houses are some way off and no one would realise where it came from.

Pin now has his finger on the trigger, with the pistol pointed into a spider's nest; it is difficult to resist the longing to press the trigger, but the safety-catch must be on and he does not know how to cope with it.

Then a shot goes off so suddenly that Pin does not even realise he has fired it; the pistol jumps back in his hand, smoking and dirty all over with earth. The tunnel of the nest has collapsed; above it is a little furrow of earth and the grass is singed.

At first Pin is terrified, then delighted. How lovely it was, how good the powder smells! But then he is terrified again to find the frogs have suddenly all gone silent and not a sound is to be heard, as if that shot had killed off the entire world. Then, very far away, a frog begins to croak again, and another nearer by, and another nearer still, till the chorus starts up again and the croaking seems to Pin louder, much louder, than before. From the houses a dog barks and a woman calls from a window. Pin thinks he won't fire again, for that silence and then those sounds have frightened him. But he'll come back another night and nothing will frighten him then; he'll fire every round in the pistol, also at the bats and the cats prowling round the chicken-coops.

Now he must find a place to hide the pistol; in the trunk of an olive-tree; or to bury it would be better; or better still to scoop out a hole in the grassy bank where the spiders' nests are and cover it over with mould and grass. Pin begins scooping away with his hands at a part where the earth is already honeycombed with tunnels made by the spiders, takes the pistol off its belt and puts it into the holster, and covers it all over with mould and grass and bits from the walls of chewed grass made by the spiders. Then he sets off back along the little channels running above the torrent-bed, with narrow lines of stones to walk on.

As he goes along Pin is dangling the end of the belt in the water and whistling so as not to hear the chorus of frogs which seems to be increasing every moment.

Now he is among the little gardens and the rubbish dumps outside the houses. As he reaches them he hears voices, not talking in Italian. Pin often goes round at night in spite of the curfew and the patrols don't say anything to him because he's only a child. But this time he is afraid, as it occurs to him that those Germans there may be looking for the person who fired a gun. They come towards him and he tries to run away; but they shout something and catch him up. Pin takes up a position of defence, holding the belt as if it were a whip. But that is what the Germans are looking at, it's the belt they are after; and suddenly they take him by the scruff of the neck and drag him off. Pin talks ceaselessly; begs, complains, insults, but the Germans do not understand any of it; they are worse, much worse, than the municipal guards.

The alley is crowded with armed German and Fascist patrols, and men they have arrested, including Michel the Frenchy. Pin has to pass through these on his way up the alley. It is very dark; the only light comes from the top of the steps, from a lamp that only lets out a glimmer because of the black-out.

By the light of the glimmer, at the top of the alley, Pin sees the sailor, his fat face distorted with fury, pointing a finger at him.

CHAPTER THREE

YES, THE Germans are worse than the municipal guards. With the guards Pin could at least, if nothing else, begin joking, and say: "If you let me go I'll arrange for you to go to bed free with my sister."

But the Germans cannot even understand what he says, and the Fascists are men he has never seen before, men who do not even know who his sister is. Both are strange types; the Germans are as rosy, fleshy, and hairless as the Fascists are black, bony, and bluish in the face, with rat-like moustaches.

Next morning, at the German headquarters, Pin is the first to be interrogated. He is faced by a German officer with a baby-like face, and a Fascist interpreter with a little beard. In a corner is the sailor, and, sitting near him, Pin's sister. They are all looking bored; the sailor seems to have made up a long story about the stolen pistol, so as not to get any blame for letting it be stolen, and must have told a lot of lies.

On the officer's table is lying the belt, and the first question Pin is asked is: "How did you get hold of this?" Pin is half asleep; he has spent the night on the floor in a passage with Michel the Frenchy near him and every time Pin was getting off to sleep Michel gave him a violent dig in the ribs with his elbow and whispered: "If you talk I'll kill you."

Pin had replied each time: "Oh, hell take you."

Michel said: "You mustn't say a word about us, d'you understand? Not even if they beat you."

And Pin replied: "Oh, devil take you."

"We've all agreed that if the others don't find me returning home they'll kill you."

And Pin replied: "I hope your soul rots."

Michel is one of those people who used to work in hotels in France before the war; he'd had quite a good time there on the whole, though sometimes they would call him *macaroni* or *cochon fasciste,* then in '40 he began being put into concentration camps and everything had gone wrong with him since: unemployment, repatriation, law-breaking.

Suddenly the sentries had noticed that Pin and Michel were talking to each other and took Pin away as he was the principal accused and was not supposed to communicate with anyone. Pin could not get off to sleep; he was used to being beaten and that did not frighten him very much, but he was in an agony of doubt about the best line to take up at the interrogation. He would have loved to revenge himself on Michel and the others and tell the Germans straight away that he had given the pistol to the men in the tavern, and also that they had formed a *Gap*; but to turn into an informer would be another irreparable action, like stealing the pistol; it would mean he would never be stood another drink at the tavern, or be able to sing or listen to dirty stories there. And then he might also involve that man Committee, who was always so glum and miserable, and Pin would have been sorry about that as Committee was the only decent man among the lot. Pin would like Committee to arrive now, all wrapped up in his raincoat, enter the interrogation room and say, "I told him to take the pistol." That would be a fine gesture, worthy of Committee, and no harm would come to him for it either, for just as the S.S. were going to lead him off to prison, there would be a shout, like at the cinema, of: "Our side's coming!" and Committee's men would rush in and set them all free.

When the German officer asks Pin about the belt he replies: "I found it." Then the officer takes up the belt and hits him over the cheek with all his strength. Pin sways and nearly falls; he feels as if bunches of needles had been stuck into all his freckles; the blood flows down his already swollen cheek.

His sister screams. Pin cannot help thinking how often she herself had hit him just as hard, and that now she's acting and just pretending to be sensitive. The Fascist interpreter leads his sister away, and the sailor begins some complicated speech in German, pointing at Pin, but the officer signs for him to be quiet. They ask Pin if he has decided to tell the truth; who sent him to steal the pistol?

"I took it to shoot at a cat, intending to bring it back," says Pin, but he cannot manage to put an ingenuous expression on his face, which feels swollen all over. He is overwhelmed by a vague longing for affection.

Another blow on the other cheek, not so hard this time, though. Then Pin, remembering his method with the municipal guards, lets out a piercing shriek even before the belt has touched him, and goes on screaming. A scene begins with Pin jumping round the room, shrieking and sobbing, and the Germans running after him trying to catch him and hit him again, while he shouts protests and insults and wilder and wilder replies to the questions they continue to ask him.

"Where did you put that pistol?"

Now Pin can tell the truth: "In the spiders' nests."

"Where are they?"

Pin, at the bottom of his heart, would prefer to be friends with these people. The municipal guards also used to hit him first, and then start joking with him about his sister. If he could make friends with these men too it would be fine to explain to them where the spiders make their nests and arouse their interest and show them all the places. Then they would all go off to the tavern together and buy wine and move on later to his sister's room to drink, smoke, and watch her dance. But the Germans and Fascists, a hairless and blueshaven lot, don't seem people with whom any undertanding is possible. They go on hitting Pin, so he will never tell them where the spiders make their nests; he has never told his friends, so why should he tell them?

Instead he begins giving great deep exaggerated sobs, like the sobs of a newborn baby, mingled with screams and curses and stamping of feet which can be heard all over the German headquarters. No, he won't betray Michel, Giraffe, Gian and the others; they are his real friends. Pin is now full of admiration for them because they are against these swine here. Michel can be sure Pin won't betray him, he must be hearing the screams and saying to himself: "He's a lad of iron, Pin is, he's holding out and not talking."

In fact the noise Pin is making can be heard over the whole building; the officers in the other rooms begin complaining; there's always a coming and going for permits and appeals at the German headquarters, and it's not good that everyone should hear a child being beaten up too.

The officer with the baby face gets an order to stop the

interrogation; he can go on another day and in a different place. But it is difficult to silence Pin now. They try to explain that it's all over, but their voices are drowned in his screams. Then a number of them cluster round him and try to calm him down, but he breaks away from them and screams louder than ever. Then they bring his sister in hoping she'll console him, and he nearly jumps up at her and bites her. After a time there's a whole group of Germans and of Fascist militiamen following him around and trying to soothe him down; one of them strokes his head, another tries to dry his tears.

Finally, exhausted, panting, breathless, Pin stops. A militiaman is now detailed to take him off to prison and bring him back next day for more interrogation.

Pin comes out of the office with this armed militiaman following him; his face looks tiny under its thatch of hair, his eyes are squeezed dry and his freckles washed by tears.

On the threshold he meets Michel on his way out, a free man.

"Hallo, Pin," says he, "I'm going home. I'm on duty to-morrow."

Pin frowns at him, his eyes red, his mouth open.

"Yes, I've asked to join the Black Brigade.[1] They've told me what the advantages are and the pay they get. Then, you know, during round-ups one can snoop around people's houses and take what one wants. To-morrow they'll give me my weapons and uniform. Keep your chin up, Pin."

The militiaman taking Pin to prison is wearing a black cap with a red *Fascio* embroidered on it. He's young and very short, with a rifle taller than himself. He's not one of the blue-shaven type of Fascists.

They have been walking along for five minutes and neither of them has yet opened his mouth.

---

[1] The Black Brigades were formed by the Fascists early in 1944 to hunt members of the Resistance.

Then, "If you want to, you can get into the Black Brigade too," the militiaman says to Pin.

"If she wants, that cow of a grandmother of yours can get into it too," Pin replies readily.

The militiaman pretends to be offended.

"Hey, who d'you think you're with? Hey, who taught you that?" and he stops.

"Go on, take me to the blasted prison, hurry up about it," says Pin.

"Why, d'you think you'll be left quiet in prison? You'll be taken off for interrogation all the time, and beaten till you're bruised all over. D'you like being beaten?"

"You, on the other hand, should go to hell."

"I'll send you to hell."

"And I you, your father and your grandfather too," says Pin.

"If you don't want them to beat you, join the Black Brigade," he says.

"And then?" says Pin.

"And then go out on round-ups."

"Do *you* go out on round-ups?"

"No. I'm stuck at headquarters."

"Liar. I wonder how many rebels you've killed and don't want to admit it."

"I swear. Never been out on a round-up."

"Except the ones you have been on."

"Except the one they captured me on."

"They captured you in a round-up too?"

"Yes, a fine round-up it was, really fine. Wiped up everyone. I was hiding in a chicken-coop. A really fine round-up, it was."

Pin is annoyed with Michel, not because he thinks Michel has behaved badly and become a traitor. What annoys Pin is to find himself making a mistake every time and never being able to forsee what grown-ups will do next. When one of them seems to be thinking in one way, Pin finds he's thinking in another; he can never foresee what the changes will be.

Pin, at the bottom of his heart, feels he'd like to be in the Black Brigade too, and go around all hung with badges and tommy-guns, terrifying people and being treated by the militiamen as one of them, linked together by the barrier of hatred separating them from other men. Perhaps, thinking it over, he *will* decide to go into the Black Brigade; at least he could get the pistol and perhaps be allowed to keep it and carry it about openly on his uniform; and then he could also get his own back on the German officer and the Fascist sergeant by making fools of them, and take his revenge in jeers for all the sobs and screams.

There is a song of the Black Brigade which goes: *And they call us the scamps of Mussolini* . . . followed by various obscenities. The Black Brigade can sing obscene songs in the streets because they are "the scamps of Mussolini"; that's wonderful, thinks Pin. But this militiaman is a fool and gets on Pin's nerves, so he replies rudely to everything he says.

The prison is in a big villa requisitioned from English owners, for the old fortress down on the port is being used by the Germans as an anti-aircraft post. It is a strange villa, in the middle of a wood of Arancaria pines, and must have looked like a prison even before, with its turrets and terraces and chimney-pots turning in the wind, and all the railings that were there before as well as those added since. The owners must have led solitary and enclosed lives in the big rooms with their wooden floors, while the wind turned the creaking chimney-pots; they must have had big dogs wandering up and down the staircases, and servants who loathed them and perhaps a daughter who would suddenly jump up from table and burst into tears, no one knew why.

Now the rooms are used as cells, strange cells with parquet and linoleum floors, great walled-up marble fireplaces,

and basins and bidets stopped up with rags. There are armed
sentries on the turrets, and on the terraces the prisoners queue
up for their rations, then scatter for their daily airing.

It is feeding time when Pin arrives, and suddenly he
realises that he's very hungry. They give him a bowl too and
put him in the queue.

Many of the prisoners are in for evading the call-up, and
also for various infringements of war-time restrictions, such
as unlicensed slaughtering of animals or trafficking in petrol
or pounds sterling. Nowadays there are very few ordinary
criminals, for no one bothers about thieves; those there have
past sentences to serve and are too old to ask to be called up
and get them remitted. The political prisoners can be dis-
tinguished by the bruises on their faces and by their awkward
movements on bones broken during interrogation.

Pin is a "political" too; it shows at once. He's eating his
soup, when up comes a big heavily-built youth with a face
even more livid and swollen than Pin's, and shaven hair
under a peaked cap.

"They've fixed you nicely, comrade," he says.

Pin looks at him, not knowing how to treat him yet.

"And you too," he says.

The youth with the shaven head says, "They interrogate
me every day and beat me up with a whip made of gristle."

He says this very grandly, as if they were doing him a
special honour.

"If you want my soup, here you are," he says to Pin. "I
can't eat it, as my throat's full of blood."

And he spits out a reddish froth on to the ground. Pin
looks at him with interest; he has always admired anyone who
manages to spit blood, and would like to see someone with
tuberculosis spitting.

"Then you're T.B.," he says to the shaven youth.

"They may have given me T.B.," agrees the other im-
portantly. Pin looks at him admiringly; perhaps they'll be-

come real friends. He has also given Pin his soup and that pleases Pin very much because he's hungry.

"If they go on like this," says the youth with the shaven head, "they'll ruin me for life."

Pin says: "Then why don't you join the Black Brigade?"

The youth with the shaven head gets up then and stares at him from his swollen eyes: "Hey, d'you know who I am?"

"No, who are you?" exclaims Pin.

"Have you ever heard of Red Wolf?"

"Red Wolf!" Who hasn't heard of Red Wolf? Every time there's an attack against the Fascists, at every bomb that explodes in one of their headquarters, at every spy who vanishes without anyone knowing what has happened to him, people whisper the name of Red Wolf. Pin also knows that Red Wolf is sixteen years old and used to work at the "Todt"[1] as a mechanic; others who'd worked at the "Todt" to avoid the call-up had told Pin about him and how he wore a Russian-style cap and always talked about Lenin and how he'd been nicknamed GPU. He also had a passion for dynamite and time-bombs and had, it seemed, gone into the "Todt" to learn how to make mines. Then one day the railway bridge blew up and GPU did not appear at the "Todt" any more; he was in the mountains and came down into the town at night, carrying a big pistol and wearing a white, red, and green star on his Russian-style cap. He had let his hair grow long and now called himself Red Wolf.

And now here was Red Wolf standing in front of him, with his Russian-style cap which no longer had a star on it, his big head shaved, his eyes swollen, and spitting blood.

"Yes, are you him?" asks Pin.

"I am," says Red Wolf.

"And when did they take you?"

---

[1] The German Todt organisation was responsible for building defences, and Italian workers in it were exempted from military service.

"'Thursday on the Borgo bridge; armed and with the star on my cap."

"And what will they do to you?"

"Perhaps," he says with his air of importance, "perhaps they'll shoot me."

"When?"

"Perhaps to-morrow."

"What're you going to do?"

Red Wolf spits blood on the ground. "Who are you?" he asks Pin. Pin gives his name. He has always wanted to meet Red Wolf, to see him appear one night in the alleys of the old town, but Pin has always been a little afraid of him, because of that sister of his who goes with Germans.

"Why are you here?" asks Red Wolf, in a tone almost as peremptory as the Fascists during an interrogation.

Now it is Pin's turn to give himself airs.

"I stole a pistol from a German."

Red Wolf gives him a look of approval, then asks in a serious voice:

"Are you part of a band?" Pin says, "No."

"You're not organised? Not in a *Gap?*"

Pin is delighted to hear that word again. "Yes, yes," he says, "*Gap!*"

"Who're you with?"

Pin thinks a little, then says: "With Committee."

"Who?"

"Committee. Don't you know him?" Pin tries to put on a superior air, but it doesn't work. "A thin man, with a light-coloured raincoat."

"You're lying. The committee is made up of lots of people, and no one knows who they are. They're preparing the rising. You don't know anything."

"If no one knows who they are, you don't either."

Pin doesn't like talking to boys of Red Wolf's age because they always try to be superior and never treat him confidentially, but like a child.

"I know," says Red Wolf, "I'm one of the *Sim*."[1]

Another mysterious word. *Sim! Gap!* What a lot of words there must be; Pin wishes he knew them all.

"I know all about you, though," he says, "I know that you are also called GPU."

"That's not true," says Red Wolf, "you mustn't call me that."

"Why not?"

"Because we're not out for social revolution now, but for national liberation. When Italy's been liberated by the people, we'll nail the bourgeoisie down to their responsibilities."

"What?"

"Just that. We'll nail the bourgeoisie down to their responsibilities. The brigade commissar explained it all to me."

"D'you know who my sister is?" The question has nothing to do with what they are saying, but Pin is tired of talking of things he knows nothing about and prefers to get back to his usual subjects.

"No," says Red Wolf.

"The Dark Girl of Long Alley."

"Who's she?"

"What d'you mean, who's she? Everyone knows my sister. The Dark Girl of Long Alley."

It seems incredible that a youth like Red Wolf has never heard of his sister. In the Old Town children of six are already beginning to talk about her and telling girls of the same age what she does when she's in bed with a man.

"Hey, you don't know who my sister is. That's a good one . . ."

---

[1] *Servizio Informazione Militare* — Military Intelligence Service — the term could apply to either side.

Pin would like to call the other prisoners round and begin his usual clowning.

"I don't even look at women at the moment," says Red Wolf, "there'll be time after the rising. . . ."

"But suppose they shoot you to-morrow?" says Pin.

"We'll just see who gets it in first, them shooting me or me shooting them."

"What d'you mean?"

Red Wolf thinks a little, then leans over and whispers in Pin's ear:

"I've got a plan and if it comes off I'll have escaped by to-morrow, and then I'll make all these Fascist swine pay one by one for beating me up."

"Escape? Where to?"

"Back to the detachment. To Biondo's. And we'll organise an action that will really make them sit up."

"Will you take me with you?"

"No."

"Please, Wolfy, take me with you."

"My name is Red Wolf," says the other. "When the commissar told me that GPU wasn't a good name I asked him what I could call myself and he said 'Wolf.' Then I told him that I wanted a name with something red in it because the wolf's a Fascist animal, and he said: 'Then call yourself Red Wolf.' "

"Red Wolf," says Pin. "Listen, Red Wolf; why don't you want to take me with you?"

"Because you're only a child, that's why."

From the beginning, ever since Pin and Red Wolf had talked about the stolen pistol, Pin had felt that they could become real friends. But now here is Red Wolf treating him like a child again and that gets on Pin's nerves. With other youths of Red Wolf's age Pin can at least assume superior airs by talking about women, but this subject does not seem to work with him. But how fine it would be to go around in a band with Red Wolf and make explosives big enough to blow up bridges and walk through towns firing machine-gun bursts against patrols. It might even be better than the Black Brigade. Only the Black Brigade wears a death's head as a badge, and that makes more of a show than a tricolour star.

It seems quite unreal to be standing there talking to someone who may be shot next day, to be on that terrace full of men crouching on the ground over their food, under chimney-pots turning in the wind and warders watching from turrets with machine-guns trained. It's like some enchanted play, surrounded by that park full of the black shadows of those strange pines. Pin has almost forgotten his beating, and is beginning to wonder whether it's all a dream.

Now the warders are getting the prisoners in line before returning to their cells.

"Where's your cell?" Red Wolf asks Pin.

"I don't know where they'll put me," says Pin, "I haven't been in yet."

"I'd like to know where you are," says Red Wolf.

"Why?" asks Pin.

"You'll see."

Pin is always irritated by people who keep on saying: "You'll see."

But suddenly, in the line of prisoners beginning to march away, he thinks he has seen a face he knows, knows very well indeed.

"Say, Red Wolf, d'you know that man ahead, the one who's so thin and walks in that strange way . . . ?"

"He's an ordinary criminal. Leave him alone. They aren't to be trusted, ordinary criminals."

"Why not? I know him!"

"They are proletarians without a class-consciousness," says Red Wolf.

CHAPTER FOUR

"PIETROMAGRO!"

"Pin!"

When a warder takes him to his cell and opens the door Pin gives a cry of surprise; he'd been right about the prisoner he saw on the terrace, the one who walked in that odd way; it really was Pietromagro.

"D'you know him?" asks the warder.

"Bloody hell do I not! He's my master!"

"Good. Then the whole concern is now transferred here," says the warder, and locks the door. Pietromagro had been inside a month or two, but to Pin, seeing him, it seems that years have passed. He's all skin and bone, yellow skin covered with hair hanging from his neck in flabby folds. He is sitting on a heap of straw in a corner of the cell, with his stick-like arms along his sides. When he sees Pin he raises them. Up to now Pin's only relations with his master have been shouts and blows; but now, finding him here in this state, he feels a mixture of pleasure and sorrow.

Pietromagro even speaks differently: "Pin! You here too, Pin!" he says in a hoarse, wailing tone, without any curses at all; and it's plain that he too is pleased to see Pin. He takes him by the wrists, but not in the way he always did before, to twist them; and looks at him from yellow eyes. "I'm ill," he says, "I'm very ill, Pin. These swine here won't send me to the infirmary. Everything's upside down here; the place is full of nothing but political prisoners and one day they'll end by mistaking me for a 'political' and putting me up against a wall."

"They beat me," says Pin, and shows the marks.

"Then you're a 'political' too," exclaims Pietromagro.

"Yes, yes," says Pin. "A political."

35

Pietromagro thinks this over. "Of course, of course, a 'political.' I'd begun to think, seeing you here, that you'd started a career as a jail-bird. For when once one gets into prison one's never away from it long; as soon as one's freed one falls back in again. But of course if you're a 'political' it's a different thing. Why, if I'd known more as a young man I'd have become a 'political' too. Ordinary crimes don't get one anywhere; steal a little and one goes to prison, steal a lot and one has villas and palaces. But commit a political crime, and though one goes inside just the same, it's at least with a hope of a better world, without prisons, one day. That's what I was told by a 'political' who was in prison with me years ago, a man with a black beard. He's dead now. For I've known every kind of convict, ordinary ones, smugglers, tax-evaders; but I've never known any as decent as the 'politicals.' "

Pin cannot quite grasp the meaning of this speech but he feels sorry for Pietromagro and stands quietly looking at the veins swelling and ebbing on his neck.

"Now, you see, I'm ill. I need treatment, instead of which here I am lying on the ground. I haven't blood running in my veins any more, but urine. I can't drink wine, and I long to get drunk for a week. The penal code's all wrong, Pin; it lists everything one mustn't do in life, stealing, murdering, receiving stolen goods, but it doesn't say a word about what one *should* do instead of all that, when one finds oneself in certain situations. Pin, are you listening to me?"

Pin looks at his shaggy yellow face, and feels his breath panting over him.

"Pin, I'm going to die. You must swear to do something. Say 'I swear' to what I'm going to say. 'I swear that I'll fight all my life long to do away with prisons and to rewrite the penal code.' Now say 'I swear.' "

"I swear," says Pin.

"Will you remember, Pin?"

"Yes, Pietromagro," says Pin.

"Now come and help me catch my lice," says Pietromagro. "I'm full of them. D'you know how to crack 'em?"

"Yes," says Pin. Pietromagro begins looking inside his shirt, then hands Pin a corner of it.

"Have a good look in the seams," he says. Catching Pietromagro's lice is not much fun, but Pin feels sorry for the poor man, with his veins full of urine and without perhaps much longer to live.

"And the shop, how's the shop going?" asks Pietromagro. Neither apprentice nor master has ever liked his job much; but now they begin discussing the work still to be done, the price of leather and thread, and who will mend shoes for the neighbourhood now that both of them are in prison. Soon they are sitting on the straw in a corner of the cell, cracking lice and talking about welting and soling, without ever abusing their jobs, which has never happened in their whole lives.

"Say, Pietromagro," exclaims Pin, "why don't you set up as a cobbler in prison, to mend the warders' shoes?"

This has never occurred to Pietromagro, who used to go to prison quite willingly once so as to eat without working. But now he rather takes to the idea; perhaps if he worked he wouldn't feel so ill.

"I can ask. Will you come in on it?"

Yes, Pin will come in on it; working in these circumstances would be something new, something they had thought up for themselves, as amusing as a game. And being in prison wouldn't be too unpleasant, with Pietromagro who wouldn't hit him any more, and singing songs to the prisoners and wardens.

At that moment a warder opens the door, and outside is Red Wolf, who is pointing at Pin and saying: "Yes, that's the one I mean."

The warder calls him out and locks up the cell, leaving Pietromagro all alone inside. Pin cannot understand what they want.

"Come along," says Red Wolf, "you must give me a hand with carrying down a barrel of refuse."

Just along the passage, in fact, there stands an iron barrel full of refuse. Pin thinks how cruel it is to make Red Wolf, who is in such a bad state from his beatings, do heavy work with only a child like himself to help him. The barrel is so high it reaches Red Wolf's chest and so heavy it's difficult to lift. While they are trying to lift it Red Wolf brushes Pin's ear with his lips and whispers: "Now keep a sharp look-out, this is our chance," then out loud: "I've been asking for you all round the cells, I need your help."

This is wonderful, Pin thinks, he never dared hope for such a thing. But Pin soon gets attached to places he is in, and even prison, he finds, has its attractions; perhaps he would like to escape with Red Wolf a little later, when he's spent a little time here, but not just when he's arrived.

"I'll do it by myself," says Red Wolf to the warders, who are helping him lift the barrel on his shoulders. "I just need the boy to steady it behind so it doesn't tip over."

They start moving, with Red Wolf bent double under the weight and Pin holding the iron barrel straight by one end.

"D'you know the way?" the warders shout after him. "Careful not to fall down the stairs."

As soon as Red Wolf has turned the first landing he asks Pin to help him rest the barrel on a window-ledge. Is he already tired? No, Red Wolf wants to talk to him. "Now listen carefully. When we reach the lower terrace you're to go ahead and begin talking to the sentry. You must hold his attention so that he doesn't take his eyes off you; you're small and he'll have to keep his head down to talk to you, but don't get too near him, you understand?"

"And what will you do?"

"I'll put a helmet on him. Mussolini's helmet. You'll see. D'you understand what you're to do?"

"Yes," says Pin, who has not understood anything yet, "and what then?"

"I'll tell you later. Just a moment. Open your hands."

Red Wolf pulls out a piece of soap and rubs it over the palms of Pin's hands, then over his legs, particularly inside the knees.

"Why?" asks Pin.

"You'll see," says Red Wolf, "I've studied my plan in every detail."

Red Wolf belongs to the generation brought up on strip-cartoons; he has taken them all seriously and life has not disproved them so far. Pin helps him lift the barrel back on to his shoulder, then when they reach the terrace, goes on ahead to talk to the sentry.

The sentry is standing by a balustrade, looking sadly over the trees; Pin goes toward him with his hands in his pockets, feeling in his element again; his old spirits of the Alley return.

"Hallo," says he.

"Hallo," says the sentry.

It's a face Pin has never seen before; a sad southerner with cheeks all hacked about from shaving.

"Hell, who do I see?" exclaims Pin. "I was just saying to myself, where's that old bastard got to, when I see you there in front of me."

The sad southerner looks at him, trying to prise open his half-shut lids. "What? Who're you?"

"Hell, you're not going to tell me you don't know my sister?"

The sentry mutters something about not knowing anyone. "Are you a prisoner? I can't talk to prisoners."

And Red Wolf hasn't arrived yet!

"Don't you tell me . . ." says Pin. "You mean to say that since you've been here you've never had a dark girl with frizzy hair?"

The sentry looks perplexed.

"Yes, as a matter of fact, I have. What about her?"

"A girl who lives in an alley round the corner of the right of a square behind a church then up some steps?"

The sentry blinks. "What?"

Pin is thinking: "It looks as if it'll turn out he really has been with her!"

"I'll just explain," says Pin. "D'you know where the market square is?"

"Mmmm . . ." says the sentry, and begins looking away; it's not working, he must find something more interesting, but if Red Wolf doesn't arrive soon everything will be wasted.

"Wait," says Pin. The sentry turns his eyes back at him for a moment.

"I've got a photograph in my pocket. I'll show it to you in a minute. Only a bit of it, though. Just the head or you won't sleep to-night."

The sentry is now leaning over him, and has even suc-ceeded in completely opening both eyes, the eyes of some cave-dwelling animal. Then finally Red Wolf appears at the entrance to the terrace; although bent double under the barrel of refuse, he is managing to walk on the tips of his toes. Pin pulls both hands out of one of his pockets and waves them in the air, as if he were concealing something: "Ih! Ih. You'd like to see it, eh?"

Red Wolf is drawing nearer, with long silent steps. Then he begins to slide one hand over the other, very slowly. Red Wolf is now right behind the sentry. The sentry is looking at Pin's hands; they are soapy; why? Then all of a sudden a stream of refuse falls on the sentry's head; and not only refuse, but something hard comes crashing down all round him; he's suffocating, he can't free himself; he's caught, and his rifle with him. Then he falls down and feels himself turning and rolling along the terrace.

Meanwhile Red Wolf and Pin have already jumped over the balustrade.

"There," Red Wolf says to Pin, "hang on there and don't let go," and he points at a drain-pipe. Pin is frightened, but Red Wolf has already almost flung him out into the empty air, and he is forced to grip the drain-pipe. Now he is slithering on his soapy hands and knees; it's rather like sliding down bannisters, only much more frightening; whatever he does he mustn't look down or let go of the drain-pipe.

Red Wolf on the other hand has leapt out into space. Is he trying to kill himself? No, he's trying to reach the branches of a pine-tree not far away, and hang on to them. But the branches break off in his hands and he falls with a crash of twigs and a shower of pine-needles. Pin feels the ground getting nearer beneath him, and is not sure if he is more frightened for himself or for Red Wolf, who might have killed himself. He touches the ground, nearly breaking his legs, and there at the foot of the pine-tree sees Red Wolf lying on the ground under a heap of little branches.

"Wolfy. Are you all right?" he calls.

Red Wolf raises his face, and the bruises from his interrogation are now indistinguishable from those of his fall. He glances around. There is a sound of firing.

"Run for it." says Red Wolf.

He gets up and begins running, with a limp.

"Run for it," he repeats. "This way!"

Red Wolf knows where to go and leads Pin through the abandoned park, full of wild creepers and spiky weeds. Shots are fired at them from the tower, but the park is so thick with trees and bushes that there is cover everywhere. Even so Pin is not quite sure if he has been hit or not, as he knows one doesn't feel a wound at once, then suddenly one drops down dead. Red Wolf leads him through a little gate, behind a greenhouse, then makes him climb a wall.

Suddenly the shadows of the park dissolve, and before them opens a scene in brilliant light and primary colours, like a child's transfer. They have a moment of panic and drop to the ground; in front of them stretches a bare hillside, and all round it, vast and calm, the sea.

Then they go into a field of carnations, crawling through them so as not to be seen by women in big straw hats watering among the geometric patterns of grey stalks. Behind a big cement water-tank near a pile of folded mats used to cover the carnations in winter to prevent them freezing, there is a hollow.

"In there," says Red Wolf. They crouch down behind the water-tank and pull the mats round them so that they can't be seen.

"We'll have to wait here till dark," says Red Wolf.

Pin suddenly remembers himself hanging on the drain-pipe and the sentries shooting, and goes into a cold sweat. Such things are almost more terrifying to remember than to live through; but one can't feel really frightened with Red Wolf near. It's wonderful to be sitting with him behind the water-tank; like playing hide-and-seek; except that there is no difference between the game and real life, and it has to be played seriously, which Pin likes.

"Are you hurt, Red Wolf?"

"Not much," says Red Wolf, passing a finger wet with saliva over his cuts. "The branches broke my fall when they cracked off. I had it all thought out. How did you get on, with that soap?"

"Bloody hell, Red Wolf, you really are amusing. How d'you know all these things?"

"A Communist must know everything," replies the other. "A Communist must know how to act in all situations."

He's amazing, thinks Pin, a pity he always gives himself such airs.

"There's only one thing I'm sorry about," says Red Wolf. "Being unarmed. I'd give anything for a Sten."

Sten; another mysterious word; *Sten, Gap, Sim,* how can he ever remember them all? But this last remark of Red

Wolf's has filled Pin with delight; now he can give himself airs too.

"I'm not worried about that myself," says he, "I've got a pistol and no one else can touch it."

Red Wolf frowns at him, trying not to show too much interest.

"You've got a pistol?"

"Hm, hm," says Pin.

"What calibre? What make?"

"A real pistol. A German sailor's. I stole it from him. That's why I was put inside."

"Tell me what it's like."

Pin tries to explain, and Red Wolf describes every existing type of pistol and decides that Pin's is a P.38. Pin is enthusiastic; pee thirty-eight, what a lovely name, pee thirty-eight!

"Where've you got it?" asks Red Wolf.

"In a certain place," says Pin.

Pin has to decide now whether or not to tell Red Wolf about the spiders' nests. Red Wolf is certainly an amazing fellow who can do all kinds of extraordinary things; but the place where spiders make their nests is a very great secret and must be kept among real close friends. Pin is not sure, in spite of everything, if he really likes Red Wolf; he is too different from all the others, grown-ups and boys too; he is always saying serious things and takes no interest in his sister. But in spite of that, if Red Wolf took an interest in the spiders' nests, Pin would like him very much. Pin, in his heart, cannot understand why all grown-up men concern themselves so much with his sister, who has teeth like a horse and arm-pits full of black hair; but grown-ups never seem to talk to him without making some remark about her, and Pin has become convinced she must be important and that he himself is important because he's the brother of the Dark Girl of Long Alley. But he is sure too that the spiders' nests are more interesting than his sister and than all this male and female business, though he can never find anyone else who realises it; if he did find someone he would even forgive a lack of concern in the Dark Girl.

"I know a place," he says to Red Wolf, "where spiders make their nests."

"*I* want to know," replies Red Wolf, "where you've got the P.38."

"Well, it's there," says Pin.

"Describe it to me."

"D'you want to know what spiders' nests are like?"

"I want that pistol."

"Why? It's mine."

"You're only a child, interested in spiders' nests, what can you do with a pistol?"

"It's mine, hell, and if I want to I'll throw it in the river."

"You're a capitalist," says Red Wolf. "Capitalists reason like that."

"Oh, go and hang yourself," says Pin.

Red Wolf says, "You're mad to talk so loud. If they hear us we're done."

He moves away from Red Wolf and they lie there in silence for a time. No, it's hopeless, Pin thinks, Red Wolf has saved him from prison, but they can't ever make friends. But he is frightened of being left alone, and this business of the pistol binds him with a double link to Red Wolf, so he mustn't burn his boats.

Now he sees that Red Wolf has found a piece of charcoal and is beginning to write something on the cement side of the water-tank. Pin also takes up a bit of charcoal and begins drawing dirty pictures; once he had covered all the walls of the Alley with such dirty drawings that the parish priest of San Giuseppe complained to the *Comune* and made himself a laughing-stock. But Red Wolf is intent on his writing and takes no notice of him.

"What are you writing?" asks Pin.

"Death to Nazis and Fascists," says Red Wolf. "We mustn't waste our time. Here's a chance to do a little propaganda. Take some charcoal and write too."

"I *have*," says Pin, and points to his obscene drawings. Red Wolf is furious and begins to rub them out.

"You mad? Fine propaganda that'll make."

"But what's the use of making propaganda here? Who d'you think will come and read anything here except lizards?"

"Shut up. I thought of putting arrows on the water-tank, then on the wall, as far as the road. People will follow the arrows to here and read this."

This is another of the games which only Red Wolf knows how to play; they are very complicated and absorbing games, but they don't make one laugh.

"What shall I write then? 'Long Live Lenin'?"

Years ago in the Alley there had been some writing which appeared continuously on a wall and went: Long Live Lenin. The Fascists came to rub it out and it was back again next day. Then one day they arrested Fransè the carpenter and the writing never appeared again. People said Fransè had died on an island.

"Write: 'Long Live Italy,' 'Long Live the Allies,'" says Red Wolf.

Pin does not enjoy writing. At school the mistress — how crooked her legs were, seen from under the bench — used to hit him over the fingers. The W for "Long Live" is very difficult to write properly: better find some easier word. Pin thinks a moment, then begins: H-E-L-L.

*   *   *

The day is beginning to lengthen and dusk never seems to come. Every now and again Red Wolf looks at one of his hands; it acts as a watch; every time he looks at it he sees it getting darker; when he can only see a black shadow it will

mean that it's dark enough for them to come out. He and
Pin have made up their quarrel and Pin has decided that he
will take him to the path of the spiders' nests, to dig the pistol
up. Red Wolf gets to his feet; it's dark enough now. "Are
we going?" asks Pin.

"Wait," says Red Wolf, "I'll go and have a look around
and then come back for you. One is less dangerous than two."

Pin doesn't want to stay alone, but he is also afraid of
coming into the open without knowing what's there.

"Say, Red Wolf," he exclaims, "you won't just leave me
alone here?"

"Trust me," says Red Wolf, "I'll give you my word to
come back. Then we'll go and look for the P.38."

Now Pin is all alone, waiting. With Red Wolf no longer
there every shadow takes on a strange shape, every noise sounds
like a footstep coming nearer. It's the sailor cursing in German
at the top of the Alley and now coming to look for him, naked
except for his vest, and saying that Pin has also stolen his
trousers. It's the baby-faced officer with a police-dog on a
lead, whipping it with the belt of the pistol. The face of the
police-dog is like that interpreter's with the rat-like moustache.
They have got to a chicken-coop and Pin is afraid he is hiding
inside there. But they go in, and find the militiaman who took
Pin off to prison, crouching down like a chicken, for some
unknown reason.

Then Pin thinks that a familiar face is peering into his
hiding-place and smiling at him. It's Frenchy Michel! But
Michel puts his cap on and his smile changes into a nasty grin;
it's the cap of the Black Brigade with the death's head on it!
Now Red Wolf is coming at last! But no, a man with a light-
coloured raincoat joins Red Wolf, takes him by an elbow and
shakes his head, pointing at Pin, with a dissatisfied look; it's
Committee! Why doesn't he want Red Wolf to join him?
Committee points at the drawings on the water-tank, huge
drawings representing Pin's sister in bed with a German.

Behind the tank there is a heap of manure. Pin had not noticed it before. Now he tries to scoop himself out a hiding-place in the middle of the manure, but as he does so he touches a human face; a man is buried alive in the manure, it's the sentry with the sad face and the cheeks hacked about from shaving!

Suddenly, with a start, Pin wakes up. How long has he been asleep? Around him now it is deep night. Why has Red Wolf not returned yet? Has he met a patrol and been captured? Or can he have returned and called him as he slept and then gone off thinking Pin was no longer there? Or perhaps there was a search for them both going on in the country around, and Red Wolf could not move a step?

Pin comes out from behind the water-tank. The croaking of frogs seems to echo from the great wide throat of the sky, the sea to be a huge shining sword in the depths of the night. Being out in the open gives Pin a strange sense of smallness, not of fear. He is alone now, alone in the whole world. He walks off through the serried rows of carnations and of *calendule,* then makes for the higher slopes of the hills, to keep above the military area. Later he will come down to the river-bed and the parts which are his own.

He's hungry. The cherries are ripe at this season. Here's a tree, far from any house. Has it grown there by magic? Pin climbs up into the branches and begins to pick the cherries carefully. A big bird takes flight almost in his hands; it was sleeping in the branches. Pin at that moment feels a friend of everything and wishes he had not disturbed it.

When he has taken the edge off his hunger he fills his pockets with cherries and climbs down from the tree, then walks on again spitting out cherry-stones. Then he thinks the Fascists might follow the track of the stones and catch him up. But no one in all the world would be clever enough to think of a thing like that, no one except Red Wolf! He decides to drop a cherry-stone every twenty yards. There, he'll eat a cherry the other side of that wall, then another past that old olive-press, and another after the medlar tree; and so on until he reaches the path of the spiders' nests. But long before he has reached the river-bed the cherries are finished. Then Pin realises that Red Wolf will never find him again.

Now he is walking along in the bed of the torrent, which is almost dry, among big white stones and bamboos rustling like paper. Down at the bottom of the wells are sleeping eels as long as human arms, to be caught by hand, sometimes, when drawing water. Where the torrents join in the Old Town, shut up now like a pine-cone, sleep drunken men and women satiated with love-making. Pin's sister is asleep alone or perhaps in company; she has already forgotten him, no longer wonders if he is alive or dead. Lying awake, dying, all alone on the straw of his cell, is Pin's master, Pietromagro, the blood turning yellow with urine in his veins.

Pin has now reached his own part; there is the irrigation channel, there is the path with the nests in it. He recognises the stones, he looks to see if the earth has been disturbed. No, nothing has moved. He scoops with his hands, almost forcing his eagerness; touching the holster gives him a soothing sensation, like a baby feeling a toy under its pillow. He takes the pistol out and passes his finger over the hollows to take the earth out. Out of the barrel, very quickly, jumps a spider; it had made itself a nest inside!

It's lovely, his pistol is, the only thing he has in all the world now. He grasps it and imagines he is Red Wolf, tries to think what Red Wolf would do if he had this pistol in his hand. But that reminds him that he is alone, and that he can't go to anyone for help, neither to those double-faced incomprehensible men at the tavern nor to his traitress of a sister nor even to Pietromagro in prison. He doesn't even know what to do with that pistol, nor how to load it; if he's found with it in his hand they'll certainly kill him. He puts it back in its holster and covers it with stones and earth and grass again. Now there is nothing left for him to do but wander aimlessly about the countryside.

He begins walking along the irrigation channels again; in the dark it's easy to lose one's balance on them and put a foot in the water or fall into the strip beneath. Pin concentrates every thought on keeping his balance; it may, he thinks, hold in the tears pressing at the back of his eyes. But the tears well over and cloud his pupils and soak his eyelashes. First they flow silently, then pour down, while sobs hammer at the back of his throat. As he walks along crying like that, a big human shadow comes towards him along the channels. Pin stops, and the man stops too.

"Who goes there?" says the man.

Pin does not know what reply to make, his tears are welling up more than ever and now he's broken into deep, desperate sobbing.

The man comes nearer; he is large and tall, dressed in civilian clothes and armed with a tommy-gun, and has a cloak strapped to his back.

"Hey, why are you crying?" he says.

Pin looks at him; he is a huge man with a flat face like one of those masks which spout water in fountains; he has spreading moustaches and very few teeth.

"What're you doing here, at this time of night?" says the man. "Are you lost?"

The oddest thing about the man is his cap, a woollen one with an embroidered edge and a pom-pom at the top, of some indistinguishable colour.

"You *are* lost. I can't take you back home, as I've nothing to do with any homes nowadays and can't take lost children back to theirs!"

He says all this almost in a tone of self-justification, more to himself than to Pin.

"I'm not lost," says Pin.

"Well, what are you doing wandering about here?" says the big man with the woollen cap.

"First you tell me what you're doing."

"Fine," says the man, "you're a bright lad, you are. As you're so bright, why are you crying? I go round at night, killing people. Are you afraid?"

"No. Are you a murderer?"

"There, you see, not even children are afraid any more of men who go around killing people. No, I'm not a murderer, but I kill people all the same."

"Are you going to kill someone now?"

"No. I'm on my way back."

Pin is not frightened of him, for he knows that some men who kill others are good fellows all the same; Red Wolf is always talking about killing and yet he is a good fellow; the painter who lived opposite killed his wife and yet he was a good fellow; Michel the Frenchy has probably killed people by now and yet he will always be the same Frenchy Michel! Then the big man with the woollen cap begins talking about killing, in a sad voice as if he did it as a penance.

"D'you know Red Wolf?" asks Pin.

"Of course I do. Red Wolf is one of Biondo's lot. I'm with Dritto. How d'you know him?"

"I was with him, with Red Wolf, and I've lost him. We escaped from prison. We shoved a barrel over the sentry. First they beat me with the belt of the pistol. I'd stolen it from the sailor who goes with my sister. My sister is the Dark Girl of Long Alley."

The big man with the woollen cap is passing a finger over his moustaches. "Yes . . . yes . . . yes . . . yes . . ." he says, trying to understand the story all at once. "And now where d'you intend going?"

"I don't know," says Pin. "Where are you going?"

"I'm going to the camp."

"Will you take me with you?" says Pin.

"Come along. Have you had anything to eat?"

"Cherries," says Pin.

"All right. Here's some bread," and he pulls a piece of bread out of his pocket and hands it to Pin.

They set off and walk through an olive-grove. Pin chews the bread; a tear or two is still falling over his cheek and he swallows it with the bread. The big man has taken him by the hand; it's a huge hand, warm and soft, and seems made of bread too.

"Well! now, let's see what happened. . . . Behind it all, you said, there was a woman. . . ."

"My sister. The Dark Girl of Long Alley," says Pin.

"Of course, behind all the stories with a bad ending there's always a woman, make no mistake about that. You're young, just listen to what I tell you. War's all due to women. . . ."

CHAPTER FIVE

PIN AWAKES to see such bright stretches of sky between branches of woodland trees that it almost hurts him to look up. It is day, a day serene and free, with birds singing.

The big man is standing beside him rolling up the cloak which he has just taken off Pin's back.

"Quick, let's be off, it's day," he says. They had walked almost all night, clambering up through olive-groves, then scrub-land, and eventually into dark pine-woods. They had seen owls, too; but Pin was never afraid because the big man with the little woollen cap always held his hand.

"You're dropping with sleep, sonny," the big man had said, as he pulled him along behind him. "You don't want me to carry you, do you?"

Pin had in fact had great difficulty in keeping his eyes open, and would have sunk happily into the mass of ferns in the undergrowth till they covered him right over. It had been almost morning when they reached the open space near a charcoal burner's hut and the big man said, "We can halt here."

Pin had stretched out on the mossy ground, and watched, as if in a dream, the big man cover him with his cloak, then go to and fro with bits of wood, break them up, and light a fire.

Now it is day, and the big man is making water on the embers of the fire; Pin gets up and does the same beside him. Standing there he looks up at the big man's face; he has not yet seen it properly in the light. As the shadows melt away in the woods and from his eyes still gluey with sleep, Pin keeps on making new discoveries about him. He's younger than he'd seemed and his proportions more normal; his moustache is reddish-colour and he has blue eyes, gaps in his teeth and a flattened nose running across his face.

"We'll soon be there now," he says to Pin now and again, as they walk on through the woods. He does not talk much and Pin enjoys walking beside him in silence; he is a little frightened, in his heart, of this man who goes round alone at night killing people, and then is so good and protective with him. Pin has always been embarrassed by good people; he does not know how to treat them and always longs to make fun of them and see how they react. But he feels different with the big man with the woollen cap, for he's a person who has done a lot of killing and can allow himself to be good without regrets.

The big man talks about nothing but how endless the war is and how after seven years with the Alpine troops he still has to go round with a gun and how the only people who are well-off these days are the women and how he'd been round every country and realised that women everywhere are all thoroughly bad lots. Most of this does not interest Pin, it's the sort of thing everyone says these days; but he has never heard anyone talk like that about women before, and thinking it over he finds he agrees with the big man. It's not as if this man is like Red Wolf who just isn't interested in women; he seems to know them well, but has realised what Pin has always realised; that they're a foul lot and that it's impossible to understand what pleasure men get from being with them.

Now they have left the pines behind and are walking through chestnut woods.

"Very soon now," says the big man, "we really will be there."

And just after that they meet a mule, with no other harness but a bridle, wandering about on its own, munching leaves.

"That's not the way to let a mule out, loose like that," says the man. "Here, Corsair, here my pretty."

He takes it by the bridle and draws it along behind him. Corsair is a mangy old mule, docile and submissive. Meanwhile they have reached a clearing in the woods, with a hut in it for smoking chestnuts. There is not a soul to be seen. The man stops and so does Pin.

"What's up?" exclaims the man. "Have they all left?"

Pin realises that perhaps he ought to feel frightened, but he does not know how things are and so feels no fear.

"Hey! Who goes there!" says the man, not very loud, and slipping the tommy-gun from his shoulder.

Then from the hut appears a little man with a sack on his shoulder. He sees them, throws the sack down on the ground and begins clapping his hands. "Hallo! Hey! Cousin! It's music day to-day!" he exclaims in a cackling voice.

"Mancino!" exclaims Pin's companion. "Where the hell are the others?"

The little man comes toward them, rubbing his hands.

"Three trucks, three loaded trucks, driving up the main road. They were seen this morning and the whole battalion has gone out to attack them. Soon the music'll begin."

He is a tiny little man, dressed in a big sailor's jersey and with a cap made of rabbit fur on his bald head. Pin thinks he must be a gnome living in this hut in the middle of the woods.

The big man passes a finger over his moustache. "Good," he says, "I must go down and have a shot too."

"If you're still in time," says the little man. "I've stayed behind to get the food ready. I'm sure they'll have already put 'em out of action by midday and are now on their way back."

"You might have looked after the mule too, as you were here," says the other. "If I hadn't come across it, it'd have ended on the seashore."

The little man ties up the mule, then looks at Pin.

"And who's this? Have you had a son, Cousin?"

"I'd cut my soul out rather than have a son," says the big man. "This lad has been in action with Red Wolf and got lost."

That is not exactly the way it was, but Pin is pleased to be introduced in such a way and perhaps the big man said it on purpose to show him in a good light.

"Here, Pin," says the big man, "this is Mancino, the cook of the detachment. You must treat him with respect, as he's old, and if you don't he won't give you a full ration."

"Listen, my little recruit of the revolution," says Mancino, "d'you know how to peel potatoes?"

Pin would like to bring out some obscenity in reply, just to make friends, but he cannot think of a suitable one on the spur of the moment, and answers: "Yes, I do."

"Good, I need an assistant cook," says Mancino. "Wait and I'll go and fetch the knives," and he vanishes into the hut.

"Hey, is he your cousin?" Pin asks the big man.

"No, everyone calls me Cousin."

"Me too?"

"You too what?"

"Can call you Cousin?"

"Of course; it's a name like any other."

Pin likes this. He tries it out at once. "Cousin!" he calls. "What d'you want?"

"Cousin, what are the trucks coming up for?"

"To hunt for us, that's what they're coming for. But we'll go out and hunt them. That's life."

"Are you going too, Cousin?"

"Of course, I must go."

"Aren't you tired of walking?"

"I've been walking and sleeping with my boots on for the last seven years. When I die, it'll be with my boots on."

"Seven years without taking your boots off. God, Cousin, how your feet must stink."

Meanwhile Mancino has returned. But he is not only carrying the knives for the potatoes. On his shoulder is perched a large ugly bird, chained by a claw like a parrot, and fluttering its clipped wings.

"What is it? What is it?" exclaims Pin, who has already put a finger under its beak. The bird rolls its yellow eyes and nearly pecks him.

"Ah! Ah!" grins Mancino. "He'll have your finger off in a second! Be careful. Babeuf's a spiteful old hawk!"

"Where did you get him, Mancino?" asks Pin, who is learning more and more not to trust either grown-ups or their pets.

"Babeuf is a veteran partisan. I got him from his nest when he was tiny; now he's the mascot of the unit."

"You'd have done better to let him free as a bird of prey," says Cousin. "He's a mascot that brings worse luck than a priest."

But Mancino has put a hand to his ear and signed to them to be quiet.

"Did you hear that? Ta . . . Tata . . . ?"

They listen. Firing can be heard from down the valley. Bursts, ta . . . pum, and an occasional boom of hand grenades.

Mancino bangs a fist against his palm, with that harsh little laugh of his: "We're at it! We're at it! I say we'll wipe the lot up. We'll crack their heads open one by one."

"Well, we won't crack much if we stay here. I'm going to have a look," says Cousin.

"Wait a bit," says Mancino, "eat a few chestnuts first. There were some left over this morning. Giglia!"

Cousin raises his head with a jerk. "Who are you calling?" he asks.

"My wife," says Mancino, "she arrived last night. The Black Brigade were hunting for her down in the town."

A woman has now appeared on the threshold of the hut; she has peroxided hair and is still young, though a little overblown. Pin thinks: one would never guess Mancino was a type to have such a young wife, so refined-looking too.

Cousin is frowning and smoothing his moustache with a finger.

"Hallo, Cousin," calls the woman, "I'm a refugee up here," and she saunters towards him with her hands in her pockets; she's wearing long trousers and a man's shirt.

Cousin gives Pin a glance. Pin understands it; even up here one can't be free of these cursed women; things will end badly if they begin coming. Pin is proud to share secrets with Cousin, secrets about women, exchanged by glances.

"You've brought good weather with you," says Cousin rather sourly, looking away and pointing towards the valley, from which firing can still be heard.

"What weather could be better than this!" exclaims Mancino. "Just listen to the heavy! Listen to the row it's making! Giglia, give him a handful of chestnuts as he wants to go down."

Giglia looks at Cousin with a strange smile. Pin notices

that her eyes are green and her neck ripples like the back of a cat.

"There's no time," says Cousin, "I must go. Get the food ready. Good luck, Pin."

And off he goes, with the rolled cloak strapped to his back and the tommy-gun still in his hands.

Pin would like to run after Cousin and stay with him, but he is aching all over, and also he finds the firing down in the valley makes him vaguely apprehensive. It would also be nice to stay up here with these two. Pin wishes they really were a gnome and his wife living alone in the middle of the wood and that he was their adopted son and talked to the fairies. But the little man in the sailor's jersey has a malicious back-biting air, like the dismal evil-looking hawk he carries on his shoulder, and the little man's wife has a way of smiling to herself which the husband does not even notice. Pin would like to say to him, "Take care, Mancino. Bloody hell, if I were you I wouldn't trust that woman too much."

"And who are you, baby?" says Giglia, passing a hand over his thatch of scruffy hair, though Pin draws his head away as he has never been able to stand women's caresses; also he doesn't like being called "baby."

"Your little son! Don't you recognise me?"

"A good answer! A good answer!" croaks Mancino, rubbing the knives against each other and driving the hawk into a frenzy. "One should never ask a partisan who he is. The reply is 'I'm a son of the proletariat, my country is the International, my sister is the Revolution.' "

Pin winks, and looks at him out of the corner of his eye: "What's that? You know my sister too?"

"Don't take any notice of him," says Giglia. "He has bored everyone with his talk about perpetual revolution, even the commissars are against him. A Trotskyist, that's what they call him, a Trotskyist!"

Trotskyist; another new word!

"What does it mean?" he asks.

"I'm not sure what it means myself," says Giglia, "but it's a word that suits him: Trotskyist!"

"Stupid fool!" Mancino shouts at her. "I'm not a Trotsky-ist! If you've come up here to annoy me, you can go straight back to the town and get yourself captured by the Black Brigade!"

"Selfish swine!" replies Giglia. "It's your fault . . ."

"Stop," says Mancino, "let me listen. Why isn't the heavy firing any more?"

In fact the heavy, which has been firing continuous bursts up till now, has suddenly stopped.

Mancino gives his wife a worried look: "What can have happened? Has the ammunition given out?"

". . . or the machine-gunner been killed . . ." says Giglia apprehensively. They both stand there listening in-tently, then look at each other again and the spite comes back into their faces.

"Well?" says Mancino.

"I was just saying," Giglia begins shouting again, "that it's your fault I've had to live with my heart in my mouth for the last two months, and you still don't want me up here."

"Bitch!" says Mancino, "bitch! One of the reasons I came up here was . . . There! It's started again!"

The heavy is firing again; short bursts, with long pauses in between.

"That's better," says Giglia.

". . . one of the reasons I came up here was," shouts the other, "that I couldn't stand living with you any longer, after all I saw you getting up to!"

"Oh yes? Then what about after the war's over and the merchant-ships sail again and you'll only see me two or three times a year? . . . Hey, what are those shots?"

Mancino listens, worried: "They sound like mortars . . ."

"Ours or theirs?"

"Let me listen. There's one firing. It's theirs!"

"It's not firing. It's exploding, farther down the valley. It's ours . . ."

"Always contradicting! Curse the day I met you! Yes, they really are ours . . . all the better, Giglia, all the better . . ."

"I told you so. A Trotskyist, that's what you are; a Trotskyist!"

Pin is thoroughly enjoying himself; he feels at home. In the Alley there were quarrels between husbands and wives that lasted for whole days, and he used to spend hours under their windows listening to them without missing a single word, as if they were on the wireless; and every now and again he would intervene with some comment of his own, shouted at the top of his voice, so that the litigants would sometimes break off, then both appear at the window-sill to swear at him.

It's all much better up here; in the middle of woods, to the accompaniment of firing, and with all these new colourful words.

Then suddenly everything is calm; the battle seems to have died down; and the husband and wife are staring furiously at each other, without a breath left in their throats.

"Hell, you aren't giving up so soon?" asks Pin. "Have you lost the thread?"

They both look at Pin, then at each other to see which is going to speak, so as to contradict at once.

"They're singing!" exclaims Pin. Now from down in the valley comes the faint echo of a song.

"In German . . ." mutters the cook.

"Idiot!" shouts the woman. "Can't you hear it's *Bandiera Rossa?*"

"*Bandiera Rossa?*" the little man claps his hands and gives a twirl in the air, while the hawk tries to fly above his head with its clipped wings. "Yes; it's *Bandiera Rossa*."

He begins running down the slope, singing: "*Bandiera Rossa trionferà,*"[1] until he gets to the edge of a bluff, where he stops and listens.

"Yes. It's *Bandiera Rossa!*"

He comes running back with shouts of delight, the hawk planing behind him on its chain like an eagle. He kisses his wife, claps Pin on the shoulder, and all three take hands and sing: "*Bandiera Rossa trionferà.*"

"You see," Mancino says to Pin, "you mustn't get the idea that we were having a serious quarrel; it was all joking."

"Really," says Giglia, "my husband is a bit silly but he's the best husband in the world."

So saying she raises his rabbit-fur cap and kisses him on his bald pate. Pin cannot tell if they are lying or not, grown-ups are always so double-faced, but anyway he has enjoyed himself very much.

"Let's get down to peeling the potatoes," says Mancino, "they'll be back in a couple of hours and won't find anything ready."

They turn out the sack of potatoes and sit round peeling them and throwing them in a pail. The potatoes are cold and freeze Pin's fingers, but it's pleasant to be peeling potatoes in the company of this strange little gnome who might be good or bad, and of his wife who is even more incomprehensible. But Giglia soon stops peeling and begins combing her hair. This annoys Pin who does not like working with someone lazing in front of him. But Mancino goes on peeling the potatoes; perhaps he's used to this, it's what always happens with them.

"What's there to eat to-day?" asks Pin.

"Goat's meat and potatoes," replies Mancino, "d'you like goat's meat and potatoes?"

---

[1] Lit. "The Red Flag will triumph." This is an Italian Partisan song, and nothing to do with the old "Red Flag."

All Pin knows is that he's hungry, and he says yes.

"You cook well, do you, Mancino?" he asks.

"Hell," says Mancino, "it's my job. Twenty years, I've spent, cooking on ships; ships of every kind and every nationality."

"Pirate ships too?" asks Pin.

"Yes, pirate ships too."

"Chinese ships too?"

"Chinese ships too."

"Can you speak Chinese?"

"I can speak every language under the sun. And I know how they cook in every country under the sun; Chinese cooking, Mexican cooking, Turkish cooking . . ."

"How are you cooking the goat's meat and potatoes today?"

"As the Eskimos do. D'you like the way the Eskimos do?"

"Hell, Mancino, as the Eskimos do it! Tell me, what else have you seen?"

"Where?"

"There. Where you've been in those ships."

Pin now sees that Mancino has a drawing of a butterfly on the skin of one of his ankles, showing below his ragged trousers.

"What's that?" he asks.

"A tattoo," says Mancino.

"What's it for?"

"You ask too many questions."

*   *   *

When the first men arrive the water is just on the boil.

Pin has always wanted to set eyes on partisans. Now he is standing open-mouthed in the middle of the clearing in front of the hut, and no sooner has he begun staring at one of them than another two or three arrive, all looking different and all hung with weapons and machine-gun belts.

They might also be soldiers, a company of soldiers who had disappeared during a war many years ago and been wandering in the forests ever since without finding their way back, their uniforms in rags, their boots falling to pieces, and their beards all matted, carrying weapons which now they only use to kill wild animals.

They are tired and coated all over with sweat and dust. Pin had expected them to arrive singing; instead of which they are looking grim and serious, and throw themselves on the ground in silence.

Mancino is skipping round them like a dog, clapping his hands, and giving great hoots of laughter: "We've given 'em a good hiding this time! How did we do it? Tell me about it."

The men shake their heads; they are lying about on the straw and not speaking. Why are they so discontented? They look as if they'd returned from a defeat.

"Well? Did things go badly? Have we had many killed?" Mancino goes round saying from one to the other, without succeeding in getting a word from any of them.

Now Dritto, the commander, arrives. He is a thin young man, with eyes framed in long black lashes and curious movements of the nostrils. He goes round swearing at the men and complaining because the food is not ready.

"Come on now; what's happened?" insists the cook. "Didn't we win? If you don't tell me I won't do any more cooking."

"Yes, yes, of course we won," says Dritto, "two trucks captured, twenty Germans killed; a good haul."

He says this in a tone of irritation, as if he were being forced to admit it.

"Then did we have lots of killed too?"

"Two wounded in the other detachment. We're all intact, of course."

Mancino looks at him; he is beginning to understand.

"Don't you realise they sent us over to the other side of

thc vallcy," shouts Dritto, "so we couldn't fire a shot! They'll have to make up their minds at Brigade; either not to trust the detachment and break it up; or to consider us partisans like all the others and send us into action. Another time if we're just put on rearguard duties we won't move. And I'll resign. Anyway I'm ill." He spits and goes into the hut.

Cousin has now arrived and calls Pin.

"Pin, d'you want to see the battalion passing? Go down there, you can see the road from the edge of the ridge."

Pin plunges down through the thickets and out on the other side. Below him he sees the road, with a line of men walking along it. They look different from the others he has seen till now; brightly coloured, gleaming, bearded men, armed to the teeth, wearing the strangest uniforms; wide hats, helmets, leather jackets, bare chests, red scarves, Fascist tunics; and all their weapons are different and all of them unknown to Pin. Some pale glum prisoners also pass. Pin thinks all this is too good to be true, that it must all be due to the sun reflecting on thc dusty road.

Suddenly he gives a start; he's seen a face he knows. There's no doubt of it; Red Wolf. He calls him and they soon join each other. Red Wolf has a German weapon on his shoulder and is limping on a swollen ankle. He is still wearing his Russian cap, but now it has a star on it, a red star with a white and green circle inside it.

"Fine," he calls to Pin, "you've got here by yourself; you're a bright lad."

"God, Red Wolf," says Pin, "how on earth did you get here? I waited so long for you."

"Well, you see, when I left you I thought I'd have a look at the place the Germans park their vehicles near there. I got into a garden nearby and from a terrace I saw soldiers fully equipped and getting ready to move. I said to myself, they must be mounting an attack on us: if they're getting ready now, they'll be up our way by dawn. So I ran all the way up here to warn them, and everything's gone all right. But I twisted my ankle, the one that was so swollen when I fell that time, and now I'm lame."

"You're amazing, Red Wolf, you really are," says Pin, "but you're a swine all the same to leave me when you'd given me your word of honour."

"Honour," he says, "is due to the Cause first."

Meanwhile they have reached Dritto's camp. Red Wolf looks all the men up and down and replies coldly to their greetings.

"You've got into fine company," says he.

"Why?" asks Pin, a little bitterly; he has grown fond of these people already and does not want Red Wolf to come and take him away again.

Red Wolf whispers in his ear. "Don't tell anyone; but this is what I've heard. They send the duds to Dritto's detachment, the cast-offs from the brigade. They may keep you here, because you're a child. But if you like I can try and get you moved."

Pin does not like the idea of being kept here because he's a child; but the men he knows are not duds.

"Tell me, Red Wolf, is Cousin a dud?"

"Cousin is a man who has to be left on his own. He always goes round alone and is a good man and has guts."

Pin would like to ask Red Wolf lots of other questions: "What about Mancino? Is it true he's a *Trotskyist?*"

Perhaps, thinks Pin, he'll explain what that means.

"He's a Trotskyist, he's an extremist, the commissar of the brigade told me so. You don't agree with him, do you?"

"No, no," replies Pin. Who knows? Perhaps *Trotskyist* means something degrading.

"Comrade Red Wolf," exclaims Mancino, coming up with his hawk on his shoulder. "We'll make you Commissar of the Soviet of the Old Town!"

Red Wolf does not even look him in the face. "Left-wing Communism, an infantile disorder," he says to Pin.

CHAPTER SIX

UNDER THE trees of the wood the ground is thick with chestnut husks and dry pools full of hard leaves. In the evenings layers of mist spread between the trunks of the chestnut trees and shroud their bases, covered with the reddish sheen of moss and the bluish marks of lichen. The encampment can be sensed before it is reached, from the smoke rising above the tree-tops and the faint singing of a chorus, growing louder as one goes deeper into the woods. The hut is made of stone, two stories high, the lower story on the ground floor for animals, and the one above, made of logs, for shepherds to sleep in.

Now there are men above and below, sleeping on piles of fresh bracken and hay; as there are no windows through which the smoke of the fire on the ground floor can escape, it curls round under the slate roof and burns the eyes and throats of the men lying below. Every night the men crouch round the fire, lit under cover in case it is seen by the enemy, and crowd up together, with Pin in the midst of them, lit by flickering flames and singing away at the top of his voice as he used to in the tavern in the Alley. The men look rather like the men of the tavern too, sitting there with hard eyes and splaying elbows, though they are not gazing resignedly into purple glasses; their hands are on the barrels of their weapons and to-morrow they will be going out to fire them against other men; against the enemy!

It is this that makes them different from others, this that gives Pin a feeling new to him, that he has never felt before; it's their having enemies. In the Alley there was shouting and rowing and insulting between men and women going on night and day, but there was never this bitter longing to meet the enemy, a longing which keeps these men awake at night. Pin does not yet realise what it means, to have enemies. To

Pin there's something as disgusting as worms about all human beings; and something good and warm, too, which draws him to their company.

But these men can think of nothing but the enemy; they're like lovers; when they say certain words their beards quiver, their eyes glisten, and their hands stroke the barrels of their rifles. They do not ask Pin to sing songs about love or comic songs that make them laugh; what they want are songs full of bloodshed and violence, or others so obscene that they have to be shouted out with hatred. Yes, these men fill Pin with more admiration than any others ever have.

Below the hut the woods straggle off into strips of meadow, and there, it is said, spies are buried; Pin is a little afraid of passing that way at night, in case he feels a tug at his heels from hands growing up through the grass.

Pin is now accepted as one of the band; he is in everyone's confidence and knows the right phrase to make fun of each man, or cheer him up, or make him lash out.

"Hell, chief" he says to Dritto, "they say you've got your uniform all ready for when you go down below, with badges of rank, spurs and sword."

Although Pin jokes with the leaders, he always tries to keep on the right side of them, for he likes to be in with them in case he can get off guard duty or some other job.

Dritto is the son of emigrants from Southern Italy; he has the smile of a sick man, and lids always lowered over his long lashes. He is a waiter by profession; not a bad profession as one lives with the rich and only works alternate seasons; but he would much prefer to lie in the sun all the year round, with his thin muscular arms behind his head. Instead of which there is some demon in him which keeps him perpetually on the move and makes his nostrils quiver like antennae and gives him a subtle pleasure in handling weapons. They are doubtful about him at brigade headquarters as he has had unfavourable reports from the Committee, for he always wants to act on his own and is too fond of giving orders and not fond enough of setting an example. But he can be brave when he wants to be and there are not many men capable of leadership available; so he has been given this detachment, which is considered unreliable, and useful mainly to dump men who might harm others. Dritto is offended about this and inclined to play up to brigade headquarters; every now and again he says he is ill and spends entire days lying on the bracken in the hut, with his arms behind his head and his long lashes lowered over his eyes.

The detachment needs a good commissar to keep its leader on the right lines; but the commissar, Giacinto, is perpetually tortured by lice, which he has allowed to spread all over him and which he can no longer hold in check, so that he is beyond exercising any authority either over the commander or the men. Every now and again he is called to battalion or brigade headquarters to report on the situation and discuss means of dealing with it; but it is all wasted breath, for as soon as he gets back he starts scratching again from morning till night, and pretends not to notice what the commander is doing or what the men are saying about him.

Dritto takes Pin's jokes with a quiver of the nostrils and that sick smile of his, and says Pin is the best man in the detachment and that as he himself is ill and wants to resign they might as well put Pin in command, for things are bound to go wrong anyway. Then the men all turn on Pin and ask him when he is coming into action with them and if he can aim and fire at a German. This makes Pin angry, for in his heart he knows he would be frightened to be in the middle of shooting and is not even sure if he would be capable of firing at a man. But when they say that sort of thing to him he tries to convince himself that he is like them, and begins describing what he will do when he's allowed to go into battle, holding his fists under his eyes as if he were firing a machine-gun.

This excites him; he thinks of the Fascists and when they beat him and of these bluish and hairless faces at the interrogation; ta-tatata, they're all dead, chewing the carpet under the German officer's desk, with bleeding gums. He too feels that sharp rasping urge to kill, even to kill the militiaman hiding in the chicken-coop, stupid though he is, perhaps just because he is stupid, to kill the gloomy sentry at the prison too, gloomy though he is, just because he is gloomy and his face is all hacked about from shaving. The urge is remote, vague, like the urge to love; it has an exciting and unpleasant taste like cigarettes or wine.

"If I was a boy like you," says Long Zena, "I'd nip straight down into town, shoot an officer, then escape up here again. No one would take any notice of a boy like you and you could get right under their noses. It would be easy for you to escape, too."

Pin gets furious; he knows they say these things to make fun of him, and then won't give him any weapon or let him leave the camp.

"Send me," he says, "and I'll go, you see."

"All right, go to-morrow," they say.

"How much d'you bet that I'll go down and do in an officer, one day?"

"Come on, Dritto," says the others, "you'll give him a weapon, won't you?"

"Pin is assistant-cook," says Dritto, "his weapons are a knife for the potatoes and a ladle."

"To hell with all your weapons! Why, I've got a German naval pistol that's better than any of yours!"

"Really!" say the others. "And where d'you keep it, at home? A naval pistol; it must be one of those water ones."

Pin chews his lips; one day he'll go down and dig up the pistol, and do wonderful things with it that will astonish them all.

"What d'you bet I've got a P.38 hidden?"

"D'you think you're a partisan, keeping arms hidden? Describe the place and we'll go and fetch it."

"No, it's a place no one knows but me, and I won't tell anyone."

"Why not?"

"Spiders make their nests there."

"Oh, go on with you. Spiders never make nests. They're not swallows."

"If you don't believe me, then give me one of your weapons."

"We got our weapons for ourselves. We con-quer-ed them!"

"Hell, I conquered mine too. In my sister's room, while the other one . . ."

The others laugh, they don't understand what he is talking about. Pin feels like going off with his pistol and being a partisan all on his own.

"What d'you bet I'll find your pistol for you, your P.38?"

The question is asked by a slim youth with a perpetual cold, the shadow of a moustache, and froth congealed on his lips, called Pelle. He is polishing the bolt on a gun, with a rag, very carefully.

"I'll bet your blasted uncle you'll never find the place where spiders make their nests," says Pin.

Pelle stops rubbing a second. "Silly, I know that river-bed inch by inch, you can't even guess the number of girls I've had on those banks."

Pelle's two passions are weapons and women. He won Pin's admiration by his knowing talk about the qualities of all the prostitutes in the town and by saying things about Pin's sister that suggested he knew her well too. Pin feels a mixture of attraction and repulsion for him, so thin, with that perpetual cold of his, forever telling stories about girls he has tricked into going out into the fields and then had there, or about the new complicated weapons issued to the Black

Brigade. Pelle is young but has been all over Italy camping with the Young Fascists, and he has always handled weapons and visited brothels, even before reaching the prescribed age.

"No one knows where the spiders' nests are except me," says Pin.

Pelle laughs, showing his gums. "I know," he says, "I'm going down into town now to get a tommy-gun from a Fascist's house, and I'll look for your pistol too."

Pelle goes down into the town every now and again and returns loaded up with weapons; he always seems to know where there are hidden weapons and who has them, and risks capture every time in order to increase his armoury. Pin is uncertain if Pelle is telling the truth; perhaps Pelle is the great friend he has been seeking for so long, who knows all about women and pistols and spiders' nests too; but those reddish, cold-ridden eyes of his are frightening.

"And will you bring me it, if you find it?" asks Pin.

Pelle's grin is all gums: "If I find it, I'll keep it for myself."

It is difficult to get Pelle to give up any weapons; every day there are rows at the detachment about Pelle not being a good comrade and pretending to have owners' rights over all the weapons he's acquired. He had joined the Black Brigade before going into the partisans, so as to have a tommy-gun, and had gone round the town at night shooting at cats. Then he had deserted from the Black Brigade after emptying half their armoury; since then he had always gone back to the town at regular intervals and found strange new automatic weapons and grenades and pistols there. He often talks about the Black Brigade, painting it in diabolic colours, but always with a certain fascination. "At the Brigade they say this . . . they do that. . . ."

"All right, Dritto, I'm off, as we agreed," says Pelle now, licking his lip and giving little sniffs.

The men are not supposed to go and come on their own

as they feel like it, but Pelle's expeditions are always fruitful; he never returns empty-handed.

"I'll let you go for two days," says Dritto, "not more, d'you see? And don't do anything silly and get yourself captured."

Pelle goes on licking his lips. "I'll take the new Sten," he says.

"No," says Dritto, "take the old Sten. We need the new one."

The usual question.

"The new Sten's mine," says Pelle, "I brought it here and I'll take it when I like."

When Pelle grows quarrelsome his eyes get redder still as if he were about to burst into tears and his voice becomes even more nasal and stuffed-up. Dritto, on the other hand, is cold and inflexible, and gives only a quiver of the nostrils before opening his mouth.

"In that case you don't move," he says.

Pelle begins a long complaint, boasting of his own merits and saying that if that's the way he's treated he'll leave the detachment and take all his weapons with him. Suddenly Dritto gives him a sharp slap on the face. "You do just what I tell you, see?"

The others look on, approvingly; they have no more liking for Dritto than for Pelle, but are pleased to see their commander make himself respected.

Pelle stands there with his nose in the air and the red marks of fingers showing on his pale cheek.

"You'll pay for this," he says. Then he turns and leaves.

It is misty outside. The men shrug their shoulders. Pelle has made scenes like that before and has always returned with another haul. Pin runs after him. "Say, Pelle, my pistol, listen, that pistol . . ." he calls, not quite knowing what he wants to ask him. But Pelle has vanished and Pin's shouts are muffled in the mist. He returns among the others, who have straw in their hair and sour looks.

To liven up the atmosphere and get his own back for the way they made fun of him Pin begins jeering at those least able to defend themselves and who can most easily be laughed at. He settles on four Calabrians nicknamed Duke, Marquis, Count and Baron. They are brothers-in-law, who left their own parts to come and marry four sisters from Calabria, emigrated up here; they make a group on their own, under the leadership of Duke, who is the oldest and can get himself respected.

Duke wears a round fur cap pulled down over one eye, and has straight moustaches on a square proud face. In his belt is a big Austrian pistol; this he pulls out and thrusts in the stomach of anyone who contradicts him, grunting some truculent phrase in his angry-sounding dialect, full of repetitions and strange dissonances: "I'll bbblow your bbbrains out!"

Pin copies him. Then Duke, who cannot stand being jeered at, runs after him waving the Austrian pistol and shouting: "I'll bbblow your bbbrains out!"

But Pin is taking the risk because he knows that the others are on his side and that it amuses them to make fun of the Calabrians; Marquis with a face like a sponge and hair low on his forehead; Count, dark and gloomy as a mulatto, and Baron, the youngest, with a big peasant's hat, a swivel eye and a medal of the Virgin hanging from a button-hole. Duke's job had been slaughtering for the black market and whenever there is an animal to cut up he asks to do it; there is some dark blood-cult in him. Often they go off, all four of them, down towards the valley and the carnation plantations where the sisters, their wives, live. And there they have mysterious duels with the Black Brigade, ambushes and vendettas, as if they were waging, on their own, a war caused by ancient family feuds.

Sometimes, at night, Pin is told to be quiet by Long Zena, who has reached a good part in his book and wants to read it out loud. Long Zena spends entire days without leaving the hut, lying stretched out on the dirty straw, reading a big book called *Super-Thriller,* by the light of a little oil-lamp. He has even been known to take the book into action with him and go on reading it, leaning on the magazine of the machine-gun, while waiting for the Germans to appear.

He reads out loud in a monotonous Genoese cadence; it's a story about men disappearing in the mysterious Chinese quarters of an American port. Dritto likes hearing him read and tells the others to keep quiet; Dritto has never in his life had the patience to read a book through, but once, when he was in prison, he had spent hours and hours listening to an old convict reading *The Count of Monte Cristo* out loud and had enjoyed that very much.

But Pin cannot understand the pleasure of reading and is getting bored. He says: "Hey, Long Zena, what will your wife say that night?"

"Which night?" asks Long Zena, who is not yet used to Pin's jokes.

"The first night you go to bed with her and spend the whole time reading!"

"Porcupine-face!" exclaims Long Zena.

"Bull-face!" replies Pin. The Genoese has a long pale face with two enormous lips and slanting eyes under the peak of a leather cap that's so stiff it might be made of wood. Long Zena gets angry and starts getting up. "Why bull-face? Why d'you call me bull-face?"

"Bull-face!" repeats Pin again and again, keeping out of range of his huge hands.

Pin feels he can risk this as he knows that the Genoese will never make the effort to run after him, and will always decide after a bit to let Pin go on talking, and start reading again from where his big finger is holding the place. He is the laziest man in the whole brigade; though his shoulders are like a stevedore's he always has some excuse, on marches, to avoid carrying a load. One by one all the detachments had got rid of him until he's ended up in Dritto's.

"How cruel it is," says Long Zena, "that men have to work all their lives."

But there are countries, such as America, where men can get rich without much effort; Long Zena will go off there as soon as the boats begin sailing again.

"Free enterprise, the secret of everything is free enterprise," says he, stretching his long arms lying on the straw, and following again, with a finger, the book describing life in that free happy country.

At night, when everyone is asleep in the straw, Long Zena folds back the page he has begun, shuts the book, blows out the oil-lamp and goes off to sleep with his cheek resting on the cover.

CHAPTER SEVEN

THE DREAMS of the partisans are short and rare, dreams born of nights of hunger, linked to food which is always scarce and always to be divided among so many; dreams about chewing bits of bread and putting them away in drawers. Stray dogs must have dreams like that, about gnawing bones and burying them. Only when the men's stomachs are full, when the fire is lit, and there has not been too much marching the day before, can they dream of women and wake up in the morning with spirits free and soaring, gay as if anchors have been drawn.

Then the men lying in the straw begin to talk about their women, about those in the past and those in the future, to make plans for when the war is over, and to pass each other faded yellow photographs.

Giglia sleeps by the wall, the other side of her dumpy

little bald husband. In the morning she listens to the men talking with so much yearning, and feels their glances slithering towards her like snakes in the straw. Then she gets up and goes out to the spring to wash herself. The men remain in the darkness of the hut, thinking of her opening her shirt and soaping her breasts. Dritto, who has always been silent, gets up and goes out to wash too. The men laugh at Pin for reading their thoughts.

Pin feels among them as he felt among the men in the tavern, only this world is more brightly coloured, more savage, with these nights in the hay and these beards crawling with lice. There is something else which attracts and frightens Pin, apart from that absurd fixation about women which is common to all grown-ups; every now and again they return to the hut leading some yellow-faced man whom Pin has not seen before, and who looks around as if incapable of shutting his staring eyes or of unlocking his jaws to ask something he longs to know.

The man goes docilely out with them, into the misty terraced meadows that lie at the edge of the woods; no one ever sees him return, and sometimes his hat or jacket or nailed boots appear on someone else. Pin finds this fascinating and mysterious, and he tries every time to join the little group of men walking off into the fields; but they push him away with curses, and Pin is left jumping about in front of the hut and poking a broom at the hawk, thinking meanwhile of the secret rites taking place in the misty damp grass.

*   *   *

One day Duke returns to the camp after having gone off with his three brothers-in-law on one of those mysterious expeditions of theirs. He arrives wearing a black woollen scarf round his neck and carrying his fur cap in his hand.

"Comrades," he says, "they've killed my brother-in-law Marquis."

The men come out of the hut and watch Count and Baron arriving, also wearing black woollen scarves round their necks, and carrying a stretcher made of vine poles and olive branches on which is lying the body of Marquis, killed by the Black Brigade in a field of carnations.

The brothers-in-law put the stretcher down in front of the hut and stand round it with their heads bare and their chins lowered. Then they notice the two prisoners. These are Fascist prisoners captured in an action the day before, who are standing there peeling potatoes, with feet bare and torn uniforms where the badges had been ripped off, explaining for the hundredth time to anyone near them that they had only joined the Black Brigade because they were forced to.

Duke orders the two prisoners to take picks and spades, and carry the stretcher to the meadows, to bury their brother-in-law's body. They set off; the two Fascists carrying on their shoulders the stretcher of branches with the corpse on it, followed by the three brothers-in-law, Duke in the middle with the other two on each side of him. They are holding their caps in their left hands at the level of their hearts; Duke his round fur cap, Count a woollen cap-comforter, Baron his big peasant's hat; in the other hand each of them carries a pistol, cocked. A short way behind follow all the others, in silence.

Then Duke begins reciting the prayers for the dead; the Latin words sound heavy with anger in his mouth, like curses; the two brothers-in-law intone the responses, with their pistols always cocked and their caps held to their chests. The funeral advances through the fields, at a slow pace; Duke gives the Fascists a few sharp orders every now and again, to go slowly, to hold the stretcher level, and to turn; eventually he orders them to stop and begin digging a grave.

The others also stop, some distance away, and stand looking on. The three Calabrian brothers-in-law stand near the stretcher and the two digging Fascists, their heads still bare, still with their black woollen scarves and cocked pistols, saying Latin prayers. The Fascists work quickly; soon they have dug a deep trench and look up at the brothers-in-law.

"More," says Duke.

"Deeper?" ask the Fascists.

"No, wider," says Duke.

The Fascists go on digging and throwing up earth, making a trench two or three times wider.

"Enough," says Duke.

The Fascists lower the body of Marquis into the middle of the trench; then climb out to throw earth on top.

"Down," says Duke. "Cover it from down there."

The Fascists throw spadefuls of earth up on to the dead man until they are each standing in separate ditches with the corpse between them. Every now and again they turn round to see if Duke will let them get up again, but he tells them to go on throwing earth on the body, until there is a mound above it.

Then the others leave the brothers-in-law standing there with their bared heads and their cocked pistols; and the mist comes up, a thick mist that blurs shapes and muffles sound.

*   *   *

The story of the Calabrian's funeral, when known at brigade headquarters, aroused considerable disapproval, and Giacinto the commissar was called once again to report. Meanwhile the men in the hut seem gripped by a wild exaggerated gaiety as they listen to the jokes of Pin, who, sparing the mourning brothers-in-law for that evening, has launched out against Long Zena.

Giglia is kneeling by the fire, handing bits of wood one by one to her husband, who is trying to coax up the flames; meanwhile she is following what's said and laughing and swivelling her green eyes around the room. And every time her eyes meet the shadowed ones of Dritto, she laughs and

Dritto laughs too, that evil sick laugh of his, and they gaze fixedly at each other, until she lowers her eyes and looks serious again.

"Pin, stop a bit," says Giglia, "and sing that song which goes: *Who is it knocking at my door . . .?*"

Pin leaves the Genoese in peace and begins on her.

"Say, Giglia, who would *you* like to come knocking on your door?" asks Pin, "when your husband's not at home!"

The cook raises his bald head, reddened by the heat of the fire, with the sour little laugh he gives when he is being made fun of: "What I'd like is to see you come knocking at my door, with Duke behind you waving a big knife and saying, 'I'll bbblow your bbbrains out!' "

But the attempt to bring in Duke again is a clumsy one and does not work. Pin takes a step or two towards Mancino and says with a frown and a sideways grin: "What, Mancino, you mean to say you really didn't notice that time?"

Mancino has learnt by now that it's best not to ask Pin what he means.

"No, I didn't, did you?" he replies, but gives his sour laugh, because he knows Pin won't spare him and that the others are hanging on his lips to hear what he'll come out with.

"That time after you'd been at sea a year and your wife had a baby and took it off to the foundling home and you came back and noticed nothing?"

The others, who have held their breaths till now, burst into roars of laughter and try to draw the cook on: "Oh, Mancino, what happened? You never told us about that!"

Mancino laughs too, but sourly as a green lemon. "Why?" he says to Pin. "Did you meet the child when you were at the foundling home for bastards yourself?"

"That's enough," says Giglia, "can't you say anything that isn't malicious, Pin? Now sing us that song; it's so lovely."

"If I feel like it," says Pin; "I don't work to orders."

Dritto gets slowly to his feet, stretching: "Go on, Pin, sing that song she's told you to, or out you go on guard duty."

Pin shakes the hair off his eyes and grins at him. "Hey, let's hope the Germans don't come. The chief's feeling sentimental to-night."

He is all ready to parry the expected blow; but Dritto is looking at Giglia from his shaded eyes, above the cook's big head. Pin then gets into position, with his chin up and his chest out, and begins:

Who is it knocking at my front door, at my front door?
Who is it knocking at my front door?

It is a wild haunting song which Pin learnt from an old woman down in the Alley; perhaps it was sung once by story-tellers at fairs.

'Tis a Moorish captain with all his slaves, with all his slaves,
'Tis a Moorish captain with all his slaves.

"Firewood," says Mancino, and reaches out a hand towards Giglia. She takes up a broom made of sticks, but Dritto holds a hand out over the cook's head and takes it.

Tell me, woman, where is your son, where is your son?
Tell me, woman, where is your son?

Mancino still has his hand out and Dritto is now burning the sticks. Then Giglia holds out a handful of millet leaves above her husband's head and her hand meets Dritto's. Pin is following their movements with attentive eyes as he goes on singing.

My son has gone to war and can't return, and can't return,
My son has gone to war and can't return.

Dritto has taken Giglia's hand with one of his, then seized the millet leaves in the other and thrown them on the fire; after which he lets go of her hand and they look at each other.

May he be choked by the bread he eats, by the bread he eats,
May he be choked by the bread he eats.

Pin is following every movement with sparkling eyes; he is throwing more and more into his singing at every couplet, as if his very soul were in it.

And may he be drowned by the water he drinks, by the
*   water he drinks*
And may he be drowned by the water he drinks.

Now Dritto is climbing over the cook and is near Giglia. Pin's voice thunders in his throat as if it would crack open.

May he be swallowed by the earth he treads, by the earth
*   he treads,*
May he be swallowed by the earth he treads.

Dritto is now crouching down by Giglia's side; she is handing him bits of wood and he is putting them on the fire. The others are all intent on the song, which has reached its most dramatic point.

Woman, what are you saying, for I am your son, for I am
*   your son;*
Woman, what are you saying, for I am your son!

The flames on the fire are too high now; some of the wood should be taken off, not more put on, or the hay on the floor above will catch fire. But Giglia and Dritto are still passing each other twigs and leaves.

Forgive me, son, for speaking bad of you, for speaking
   bad of you,
Forgive me, son, for speaking bad of you.

Pin is sweating from the heat, and trembling all over with the effort he is making; the last high note was so piercing that a flapping and raucous screech can be heard from under the dark roof; the hawk Babeuf has woken up.

He drew out his sword and cut off her head, cut off her
   head,
He drew out his sword and cut off her head.

Mancino has now put his hands on his knees, he has heard the hawk wake and is getting up to feed it.

Off went the head and spun into the hall, spun into the
   hall,
Off went the head and spun into the hall.

The cook always has a sack by him filled with intestines of slaughtered animals.

Now the hawk is perching on one of his fingers and Mancino is feeding bits of blood-red kidneys into its beak.

On the floor of that room grew a beautiful flower, a
   beautiful flower,
On the floor of that room grew a beautiful flower.

Pin draws in breath for the last lines. He moves near Dritto and Giglia and shouts almost into their ears:

The flower of a mother killed by her own son, killed by
   her own son,
The flower of a mother killed by her own son.

Pin flings himself to the ground, exhausted. Everyone breaks into applause. Babeuf squawks. At that moment there is a shout from the men sleeping above: "Fire! Fire!"

The flames have grown into a huge bonfire, crackling and spreading over the hay covering the logs above.

"Out! Out!" The men are all stumbling about in confusion, snatching at weapons, boots, blankets, falling over others lying down.

Dritto has regained control of himself and jumped to his feet. "Quick! Clear the place! First automatics and ammunition, then rifles. Last the sacks and blankets. And remember the rations!"

The men, some of whom were lying barefoot, are seized with panic and snatching at anything that comes to hand and flinging themselves at the door. Pin plunges in between their legs and opens himself a way out, then runs to find a place from which to admire the fire. What a wonderful sight it is!

Dritto has pulled his pistol out. "No one leaves before everything's saved! Out with the things and go back! The first man I see making off I'll shoot!"

The flames are already licking the walls, but the men have got over their panic and are now leaping back into the middle of the flames and smoke to save the weapons and rations. Dritto enters too and shouts orders, coughing amid the smoke, then comes out again to call others and prevent their escaping. He finds Mancino in a bush with all his belongings round him and orders him back to the hut to get the cooking-pot.

"Anyone I don't see going back will catch it from me!"

Giglia passes him, calmly going towards the fire, with that strange smile of hers. "Go away!" he mutters to her.

He's a poor creature, is Dritto, but he has an instinct for command; he knows that the fire is his fault, due to his losing control of himself; he knows that he will certainly be in serious trouble with his superiors, but now he is a leader again, his nostrils quivering as he directs the evacuation of the hut in the middle of the fire, dominating the confused rushing to and fro of the men caught by a surprise while resting, who would have lost all the material as long as they saved themselves.

"Upstairs!" he shouts. "There's still a machine-gun there and two haversacks of ammunition!"

"Can't get up there!" they reply, "the floor's all flames."

Suddenly there is a shout: "The floor's falling in! All outside!"

Now explosions can be heard — some grenades which had remained in the straw. Dritto shouts, "All outside! Keep away from the hut! Take the stuff some way off, particularly the explosives!"

Pin, from his observation post on a mound, sees the fire break out into sudden bursts like fireworks and hears shots, even bursts of machine-gun fire, as the ammunition belts fall into the flames and explode, one cartridge after the other; from a distance it must sound like a battle. Sparks fly high into the sky, the tops of the chestnut trees seem tipped with gold; a branch first looks gilded then suddenly goes incandescent; the fire is spreading into the trees, soon perhaps it will burn up the whole wood.

Dritto is making a list of missing material: a Breda, six belts of ammunition, two rifles, lots of grenades, cartridges and a sackful of rice. He will never command again; they may shoot him; yet his nostrils are still quivering, he goes on apportioning jobs out among the men, as if this were a normal move

"Where are we going?"

"I'll tell you later. Let's get out of the woods. Come on."

The detachment, loaded with weapons and baggage, moves off through the meadows in single file. Mancino is carrying the cooking-pot with Babeuf perching on top of it Pin has charge of the other kitchen things. Now a rumour begins circulating among the men: "The Germans have heard the shots and seen the fire, we'll soon have them on our heels." Dritto turns an impassive yellow face towards them

"Silence! No one is to say a word! Come on, walk!"

He might be organising a retreat after an unsuccessful engagement.

CHAPTER EIGHT

THE NEW camp is in a barn, where they are all crowded up on top of each other; the roof has fallen in and lets the rain through. In the morning they scatter to sun themselves among the alpenroses on the rocky slopes around, lie on the frosty bushes and take off their shirts to look for lice.

Pin likes being sent off by Mancino on errands to places nearby, to fill pails for the cooking-pot at the spring, or gather wood among the burnt trees with a little hatchet, or fish out water-cress for the cook's salads from the stream. Pin sings as he goes, looking at the sky and the clear morning world and the mountain butterflies of strange colours meandering over the meadows. Every time he keeps Mancino waiting impatiently while the fire goes out and the rice gets sticky, and each time he is cursed in every language under the sun when he arrives back, with his mouth full of strawberry juice and his eyes dancing with the fluttering of the butterflies. Then Pin becomes the little boy of Long Alley again, starting rows which go on for hours and draw the men away from the alpenroses to collect round the kitchen fire.

But when he wanders along the paths in the mornings Pin forgets the old streets with their stagnant mules' urine, the odour of male and female in his sister's unmade bed, the sour smell and smoke from the broken gratings and open drains, the hiss of the belt during that interrogation. Now Pin has discovered all kinds of coloured things; yellow and brown mushrooms growing damp in the earth, red spiders on huge invisible nets, hares all legs and ears which appear suddenly on the path then leap zigzagging out of sight.

Yet a passing sudden thought is enough to draw Pin back into the squalid ambiguous world of human beings; and, with eyes screwed up and freckles clustering, he watches the crickets making love, or thrusts pine needles in the slimy backs of little toads, or makes water over an ant heap and watches the porous earth dissolve and open and hundreds of little red and black ants scurry away through the mud.

Then the world of men draws him again, of incomprehensible men with their opaque looks and angry mouths. And he goes back to Mancino, the little man whose laughter is getting sourer and sourer, and who never leaves his cooking pots to go into action but stays there perpetually talking about revolution, while the hawk flaps its clipped wings on his shoulder.

Cousin is different; although he seems to be forever complaining and hinting that he is the only one who really feels the strain of war, he still goes round by himself with his tommy-gun on his shoulder, and every time he returns to camp sets off again a few hours later, always with that reluctant air of his as if he is only doing it because he has to.

Whenever there is a mission to be carried out Dritto looks round and says: "Who wants to go?"

Then Cousin shakes his big head as if he were the victim of an unjust fate, loads his tommy-gun on his shoulder, and goes off sighing, with that gentle face of his looking more than ever like the mask on a fountain.

Dritto sprawls among the alpenroses with his arms behind his head and his gun between his knees, feeling sure that measures are being taken against him at brigade headquarters. The men's eyes are heavy with sleep above their matted beards; Dritto tries not to look at them as he feels their glances are full of dumb resentment against him. But they still obey him, as if by mutual agreement, to avoid drifting to disaster.

Yet he listens to everything, and every now and then gets up to give an order; he does not want the men to get out of the habit of thinking of him as their leader; if they do, even for a moment, he will have lost them.

The burning of the hut has never worried Pin; it was a wonderful fire and the new camp is surrounded by lovely places to explore. But he's a little frightened of going near Dritto; he wonders whether Dritto will try and put all the blame for the fire on to him, for distracting attention by his singing.

Now Dritto is calling him: "Pin, come here!"

Pin goes towards the sprawling Dritto, not daring to bring out any of his usual jokes; but he knows Dritto is hated and feared by the others and feels rather proud to be near him at that moment, almost as if he were an accomplice.

"D'you know how to clean a pistol?" asks Dritto.

"Well," says Pin, "you take it to bits and I'll clean the parts."

Everyone is a little nervous of Pin, as they never know what he will say, but Dritto senses that to-day Pin will not mention the fire or Giglia or any of those things, so the boy is the only member of the band he can be with.

He spreads out a handkerchief and puts the pieces down on it as he dismembers the pistol. Pin asks if he can help to take it to pieces and Dritto shows him how. Pin enjoys sitting there talking to Dritto like this, in low voices and without either saying anything disagreeable to the other. He compares Dritto's pistol with his own buried one and talks about the parts that are different or better in both. And Dritto does not make the usual comment, that he doesn't believe Pin has a buried pistol; perhaps he does believe it, anyway, and only said he didn't to make fun of Pin; Dritto seems a nice man when Pin talks to him like this, and when he's explaining how the pistol works he becomes enthusiastic and no longer looks obsessed by evil thoughts. Even pistols, when talked about like this, no longer seem instruments for killing people, but strange enchanted toys.

The other men lie about looking angry and abstracted; they take no notice of Pin wandering round them and do not want to hear him sing. It is bad when discouragement seeps into the men's bones like damp from the earth, and they no longer trust their leaders and feel they are already surrounded by Germans with flamethrowers among the rocks and alpen-roses, and that they will have to flee from valley to valley and die one by one in this never-ending war. They begin discuss-ing the war — when it started and who wanted it and when it would end, and if things would be better then or worse than before.

Pin does not know the difference between when there's war and when there isn't. He seems to have heard people talk-ing about war ever since he was born, only the bombings and the black-out came later.

Every now and again aeroplanes pass over the mountains; one can look at their undersides, without escaping into tunnels as one has to in towns. Then far away towards the sea there is a sound of bombs, and the men think of their homes which are perhaps in ruins at that moment and tell each other that the war will never end and how they can't understand who wanted it.

"I know who wanted it! I've seen them!" a man called Carabiniere suddenly says, "It was the students!"

Carabiniere is even more ignorant than Duke and lazier than Long Zena; his father was a peasant who, realising he would never get his son to wield a spade, said to him: "Join the Carabinieri"; so the son joined and was given a black uniform with a white bandolier and carried out his duties in town and country without ever realising what he was doing. After the 8th of September he was told to arrest the parents of deserters, then one day he heard that he was going to be deported himself as he was for the King; so he escaped. First the partisans had wanted to make him dig his own grave, because of those parents of deserters he had arrested; then they realised that he was just a poor wretch and had sent him to Dritto's detachment, as no one wanted him in any of the others.

"In '40 I was in Naples and I know!" says Carabiniere. "It was the students! They carried flags and placards and yelled 'Malta and Gibraltar' and that they wanted five meals a day."

Duke spits violently and touches his Austrian pistol. "The Carabinieri are all pigs, swine and bastards!" he says between his teeth. In his part of the country there is a long history of struggle with the Carabinieri, of Carabinieri shot and killed by wayside shrines.

Carabiniere protests, panting and waving his big peasant hands in front of his tiny eyes and low forehead.

"Us Carabinieri were against them! Yes, sir, we were against the war the students wanted. We tried to keep them in order! But we were twenty to one against, so they had their war!"

Mancino is standing a little way off, looking as if he's on tenterhooks; he is stirring the rice in the cooking-pot; if he stops stirring for a second it will stick. Meanwhile he can hear snatches from time to time of what the men are saying; when they talk politics he always wants to be right among them, for they know nothing, he thinks, and need him to explain everything. But now he can't leave the cooking-pot, and gives little hops of desperation, wringing his hands; "Capitalism!" he shouts now and again, "Exploitation by the bourgeoisie," as if suggesting ideas to the men, who refuse to listen to him.

"In Naples in '40," explains Carabiniere, "there were great struggles between students and Carabinieri! And if we Carabinieri had had our way there wouldn't have been a war! But the students wanted to burn down the town hall! Mussolini was forced to make war!"

"Poor old Mussolini!" jeer the others.

"To hell with you and your Mussolini!" shouts Duke.

From the kitchen comes Mancino's voice, bleating: "Mussolini! Imperialist bourgeoisie!"

"The town hall, they tried to burn the town hall! So what could us Carabinieri do? If we'd put them in their places, though, Mussolini would never have started the war!"

Mancino, torn between his duty to the cooking-pot and his longing to go and talk about revolution, is bleating away until finally he attracts the attention of Long Zena and signs for him to come over. Long Zena thinks he is being called to taste the rice and decides to make the effort to get up. Mancino shouts: "Imperialist bourgeoisie, tell 'em it's the bourgeoisie making war for its markets!"

"Oh, hell," says Long Zena and turns his back on him. Mancino's speeches always bore him to death; he can't understand them, he knows nothing about the bourgeoisie or communism, and he is not attracted by a world in which everyone has to work, he prefers one in which everyone is out for himself and is working as little as possible.

"Free enterprise," yawns Long Zena, flopping down among the alpenroses again, and scratching himself through his trousers, "I'm for free enterprise; and everyone being free to get rich by his own efforts."

Carabiniere is now explaining his conception of history; there are two forces struggling against each other, the Carabinieri, who are poor unfortunates trying to keep order, and the students, the big-shots, the *cavalieri,* the lawyers, doctors, *commendatori,* those with salaries undreamt of, even, by the Carabinieri, and who still aren't satisfied and start wars in order to get more.

"You don't understand anything!" shouts Mancino, who cannot hold out another moment and has now left Pin to look after the cooking-pot. "Imperialism is caused by overproduction!"

"Back to your cooking!" they shout at him. "And take care the rice doesn't stick this time too!"

But Mancino is now standing in the middle of them, his little body enveloped in the big sailor's jersey with its shoulders covered with hawk's droppings, waving his fists in an endless speech about financial imperialism, arms traffic and the universal revolution that will take place when the war is over, in England and America too, and the abolition of frontiers by the International and the Red Flag.

The men lie sprawled among the alpenroses, their thin faces covered with matted beard, their hair all over their foreheads; they wear odd pieces of uniform, all tending in colour towards a dirty grey; firemen's or Fascist or German tunics with the badges torn off. All of them are there for different reasons — many are deserters from the Fascist forces or freed prisoners, some are still boys, impelled by an obstinate impulse, a vague longing to go against things.

They all dislike Mancino because he vents himself in words and arguments, not in shooting; to them his arguments seem useless, as he talks about enemies they know nothing about, such as capitalists and financiers. It's rather like Mussolini expecting the Italians to hate the British and the Abyssinians, whom none of them had ever seen, and who live beyond the ocean. And the men pull the cook in among them, play hopscotch over his little curved shoulders and hit him on his big bald head, while the hawk furiously rolls its eyes.

Dritto, still a little way off, now intervenes, dangling his machine-gun against his knees. "Go and see to the food, Mancino."

Dritto does not like discussions much either; or rather he only likes to talk about actions and weapons, about the new small tommy-guns which the Fascists are beginning to use and how he would like to lay his hands on one; but what he likes more than anything is giving orders, telling the men to get under cover while he himself jumps up to fire short bursts.

"Go on, the rice is burning, can't you smell it?" shout the men at Mancino, pushing him away.

Mancino calls on the commissar for support: "Hey, Giacinto, why don't you say something? What d'you think you're doing? They're right to call this the Fascist detachment, one can't even talk politics here!"

Giacinto has just returned from headquarters, but has not yet said if there is any news; all he has done is shrug his shoulders and mutter that the brigade commissar would be passing before nightfall on inspection. After hearing this the men throw themselves down among the alpenroses once more; now the brigade commissar will soon be here to arrange everything, and it's useless to worry. Dritto also thinks it's useless to worry, the brigade commissar will tell him what his fate is to be; and he too stretches out again among the alpenroses, though more apprehensively, tearing up little bits of shrub in his fingers.

Mancino is now complaining to Giacinto that no one in the detachment ever talks to the men about why they are partisans and what communism is. Giacinto has lice clustered thick on his head and all over the lower part of his stomach little white eggs are sticking to every single hair; Giacinto goes on cracking eggs and lice between his thumb-nails with a little click, in a gesture that has now become mechanical.

"Well," he begins in a resigned voice as if he does not want to put anyone out, even Mancino, "each of us knows why he's a partisan. I was a tinker and used to go round in the country and my cry could be heard a long way off and the women would come and bring their broken cooking pots for me to mend. I used to go into their houses and joke with the servants and was sometimes given eggs and a glass of wine. Now I can't go round the country any more because I'd be arrested; and then the bombing has messed everything up too. That's why we're partisans; so we can be tinkers again and so eggs and wine can be cheap, and so we can't be arrested any more and there'll be no more air raids. And then we want communism too. Communism means there won't be any more houses where the door's banged in one's face, so one's forced to enter by the chicken run at night. Communism means going into a house and being given soup even if one is a tinker; and if they're eating pudding at Christmas then they'll give one pudding. That's what communism means. For example: here we all are so full of lice that they almost drag us about in our sleep. Now I've just been to brigade headquarters and seen they have insect powder there. Then I said, 'Fine Communists you are, you don't send this to our detachment.' So they said they'd send some. That's what communism means."

The men have listened to him attentively and with approval; these are things anyone can understand. One of them who is smoking passes his cigarette to a comrade, and another who has to go on guard promises not to cut his turn short and to stay the whole hour before calling for his relief. They all begin discussing the insect powder which is to be sent to them, if it will kill the eggs as well as the lice or if it will only stun the insects so that an hour later they'll be biting more than ever.

No one would be talking about the war any more, if Cousin did not begin speaking: "Say what you like but according to my way of looking at it the war was started by women."

When Cousin gets started on his views of women he is even more boring than the cook; but at least he makes no attempt to convince anyone and just seems to be complaining on his own.

"I was a soldier in Albania, Greece, France and North Africa," he says, "I've been in the Alpini for eighty-three months. And in every country I've seen brothels full of women with soldiers queuing up outside, and brothels for

N.C.O.s and brothels for officers; and as well as the brothels
women taking the soldiers into the fields or up to their rooms.
There they all used to be, waiting for the soldiers to come
out of barracks, and the more lice-ridden and filthy we were
the more they liked us. I let myself be persuaded once and
all I got out of it was the clap, for three months I had to lean
against the wall every time I wanted to piss. Now when one's
in a distant country and seeing no other women but those,
the only consolation is thinking of one's own home and one's
own wife if one has one, or of a fiancée, and saying to oneself,
anyway *she's* all right. Then one comes back and yes, sir, finds
the wife, while one was away, has been drawing her allowance
and going to bed with all the men around; and when I say
'one' I mean everyone, for everyone's been through that with
those filthy creatures called women."

The others know that Cousin is telling his own story,
that his wife went with everyone while he was away and had
children whose fathers were unknown.

"Even that's not enough, though," Cousin goes on, "d'you
realise why our men are always being caught by the Fascists?
Because the place is full of women acting as spies, of wives
denouncing their husbands; why, at this very moment all our
women are sitting on the Fascists' knees cleaning their guns
for them to come and kill us with."

The others are beginning to have enough of this now,
and shout at him to stop; it's one thing his being unlucky with
his wife and her denouncing him to the Germans to get rid
of him and forcing him to take to the woods, but that is no
good reason to insult everyone else's women.

"Women, women, I tell you," goes on Cousin stubbornly,
"they're behind everything. Mussolini got the idea of the
war from the Petacci sisters. . . ."

The men comment rather jeeringly on this idea; it
couldn't have been just the Petacci sisters who made Mussolini go to war.

"You see," Cousin goes on, "a woman only has to arrive in a place and . . . you get what I mean."

Now the men don't contradict him because they understand what he is referring to and want to hear how far he'll go.

". . . a woman has only to arrive in a place and some fool at once loses his head about her . . ." says Cousin. Cousin is a man who likes being friendly with everyone, but he has a sharp tongue and when he has something to say he doesn't care who he says it to.

". . . it doesn't matter when the fool is just anyone, but if he's a fool with responsibilities . . ."

The men look at Dritto; he's lying apart, but certainly listening. The men are a little afraid that Cousin may go too far and cause a terrific row.

". . . and ends up by setting fire to a house because of a woman . . ."

There, he's said it, think the men, now something will happen. It's better this way, they say, if it has to come up some time.

But at that moment a roar is heard above them and the whole sky is filled with aeroplanes. All attention shifts to them. It is a big formation of bombers; soon some town will be left gutted and smoking beneath them, while they vanish into the clouds. Pin feels the earth vibrating under the roar and thinks of the tons of waiting bombs passing over his head. At that moment the Old Town must be emptying and people crowding into the muddy tunnel. From the south comes the deep sound of falling bombs.

Pin sees that Dritto has gone up on to a rise and is looking down into the valley through his binoculars. He joins him. Dritto is smiling his evil sad smile, as he turns the lenses.

"Can I have a look too, Dritto?" asks Pin.

"Here you are," says Dritto, and passes him the binoculars.

Through a coloured confusion in the lenses gradually

appears the crest of the hills down above the sea, and a big white cloud rising. More explosions can be heard; the bombing is still going on.

"Fine, destroy everything!" shouts Dritto, clapping a hand against his palm. "My own home first! Fling it down! My own home first!"

CHAPTER NINE

TOWARDS DUSK arrive Ferriera and Kim, the commander and the commissar of the brigade. Mist is rising outside in wisps, like dust from a series of slammed doors, and in the barn the men crouch round the fire and the two from brigade. These hand round a packet of cigarettes until it is empty. They are men of few words. Ferriera is a sturdy young man, with an Alpine cap, a small blond beard, and a pair of big cold clear eyes with which he constantly glances up through half closed lids. Kim is skinny, with a long reddish face, and moustaches which he is continually chewing.

Ferriera is a workman, born in the mountains, and is cold and clear by nature; he listens to everything with a slight smile of assent and has meanwhile already made up his mind on his own — how the brigade is to be deployed, where the heavies are to be placed, when the mortars should go into action. For him partisan warfare is as exact and precise as a machine; he has taken the revolutionary impulse matured in factories up into the mountains where he was born, and his courage and cunning is now used in places every yard of which he knows.

Kim, on the other hand, is a student; he has a great yearning for logic, for certainty about cause and effect, otherwise his mind is apt to crowd at every second with unanswered questions. He has an enormous interest in humanity; that is why he is a medical student, for he knows that the explanation

of everything is to be found in the grinding moving cells of
the human body, and not in philosophic speculation. He will
become a mental specialist, a psychiatrist. People do not like
him very much because he looks them fixedly in the eyes as if
he were trying to discover the source of their thoughts; and
then he comes out suddenly with point-blank questions that
have nothing to do with the conversation, about the other's
childhood or love-life. For him also, behind human beings,
there is the great machine of class movements, the machine
that is fed by little daily gestures and in which other gestures
burn away without leaving a trace; the machine of history.
Everything must be logical, everything must be understood,
both in history and in men's minds; but there is still a gap
between one and the other, a dark area where collective reasons become individual reasons, forming monstrous deviations
and unexpected combinations. And Kim goes round the detachments every day with his slim Sten-gun hanging from
one shoulder, talking to the commissars and commanders,
studying the men, analysing the position of each one, breaking
every problem down into its component parts; "a, b, c," he
says; everything must be clear, clear in others as it is to him.

Now the men are crowding round Ferriera and Kim,
asking for news of the war; of that distant war on the military
fronts, and of the near threatening one nearby, their own.
Ferriera explains where the British have halted for months
down in the south, and the men curse the British, who only
seem capable of bombing their homes, not of advancing or
even dropping them supplies. Then Ferriera tells them the
great news of the day: a German column is advancing up the
valley, to comb the mountains; they know where the partisan
camps are and will burn houses and villages around. But at
dawn the whole brigade will move up on to the crest of the
mountains, and will also be reinforced by other brigades; the
Germans will suddenly find all the roads under a hail of fire
and will be forced to retreat.

Then the men all break into movement; their backs ripple, they clasp hands, jerk out words through set teeth; it's the battle already starting in them, their faces are already tensed in fighting expressions, their hands groping for weapons to feel the touch of steel.

"They saw the fire, that's why they're coming," says someone. Dritto is standing a little apart, the flickering flames lighting his lowered lids.

"The fire, yes, because of the fire too, of course. But there's something else," says Kim, slowly blowing out a mouthful of smoke; the men stand there silently; Dritto raises his eyes.

"We've been betrayed by one of our own men," says Kim. Then the atmosphere becomes tense, as if a wind were cutting into the men's bones; the wind of betrayal, cold and damp as a wind off the marshes.

"Who was it?"

"Pelle. He went to the Black Brigade. Just like that, on his own, without being captured. Due to him four of our men who were in prison there have already been shot. He takes part in the interrogations of anyone caught and denounces them all."

This is the kind of news that clogs the men's blood with despair, and prevents them thinking. Pelle was there with them, only a few nights before, saying: "Listen, I'll tell you an action we can carry out!" It seems strange not to hear his wheezy breathing behind them as he greases a machine-gun for to-morrow's action. Instead of which Pelle is now down there in the forbidden town, wearing a big death's head on his black cap and carrying beautiful new weapons, no longer frightened of round-ups, and driven always by that inner frenzy of his which makes him blink his cold-reddened eyes and lick his dribbling lips, a frenzy now turned against his former comrades, but without hatred or rancour, as if he were playing a game with friends in which the stake is death.

Suddenly Pin thinks of his pistol; perhaps Pelle has found it, as he knows all the paths by the river-bed from taking girls there, and now he is wearing it oiled and gleaming all over, as his weapons usually are, on his Black Brigade uniform. Or perhaps he was just lying when he said he knew the place where the spiders make their nests, and had used the story as an excuse for going down into the town to betray his comrades and get issued with those new almost silent German weapons.

"We must kill him now," the men say to each other, as if they were accepting a necessity; perhaps, secretly, they would prefer to see him return next day, loaded up with new weapons, and continue his private war with and against them in that grim game of his.

"Red Wolf has gone down into the town to organise the *Gap* against him," says Ferriera, with a slight smile.

"I'll go too," various men say. But Ferriera says that now they must concentrate on getting ready for next day's battle, which will be a decisive one. The men scatter to prepare their weapons and apportion jobs.

Ferriera and Kim call Dritto aside.

"We've had a report on the fire," they say.

"That's the way it happened," says Dritto. He has no desire to justify himself. Nothing matters now.

"Is there anyone else responsible for the fire?" asks Kim.

And Dritto says: "It was all my fault."

The two gaze seriously at him. Dritto is thinking how much he would like to leave the partisans and hide away in a place he knows of, till the end of the war.

"Have you any excuse to offer?" they ask him, with nerve-racking patience.

"No. That's the way it happened."

Now they'll either say: "Go away" or "We'll shoot you." Instead of which Ferriera says: "All right. We'll talk about this another day. How are you feeling, Dritto?"

Dritto's yellow eyes are on the ground. "I'm ill," he says.

"You must try to get really well for to-morrow," says Kim. "It's very important for you too, the battle to-morrow. Very, very important. Think it over."

They do not take their eyes off him and Dritto feels a mounting longing to let himself drift.

"I'm ill," he says, "I'm very ill."

"Now," says Ferriera. "To-morrow you must keep along the crest of Mount Pellegrino from the pilon to the second gorge, d'you understand? There you'll get orders where to move to. Keep the squads well apart; the machine-guns are to go with the gunners and riflemen so that they can move together when necessary. Every single man must go into action, without any exception, even the quartermaster, even the cook."

Dritto has followed all this with little nods of assent, and occasional shakes of his head.

"No one excepted," he repeats, "not even the cook?" and he listens attentively.

"You must all be up on the crest by dawn, d'you understand?" Kim looks at him, chewing his moustache. "Are you quite sure you understand, Dritto?"

There almost seems a tone of affection in his voice, but perhaps it's just persuasion, as it's such an important battle.

"I'm very ill," says Dritto, "very ill."

*   *   *

Kim and Ferriera are walking along the dark mountainside towards another encampment.

"Surely you see now it was a mistake, Kim?" says Ferriera. Kim shakes his head. "No, it's not a mistake," he says.

"But it is," says the commander, "it was a mistaken idea of yours to make up a detachment entirely of men who can't be trusted, with a commander who can be trusted even less. You see what happens. If we'd divided them up among the good ones it might have kept them on the right lines."

Kim continues to chew his moustache. "For my part," he says, "this is the detachment I'm most pleased with."

At this Ferriera nearly loses his calm; he raises his ice-cold eyes and rubs his forehead. "But Kim, when will you realise that this is a fighting brigade, not an experimental laboratory? I can understand your getting a scientific satisfaction from watching the reactions of these men, all arranged as you wanted them, proletariat in one part, peasants in another, then 'sub-proletariat,' as you call it. . . . The political work you ought to be doing, it seems to me, is mixing them all up together and giving a class-sense to those who haven't got it, so as to achieve this blessed unity we hear so much about . . . Apart from the military value, of course. . . ."

Kim, who has difficulty in expressing himself, shakes his head.

"Nonsense," he says. "Nonsense. The men all fight with the same sort of urge in them . . . not the same, that is . . . each has an urge of his own . . . but they're all fighting in unison now, each as much as the other. Then there's Dritto, there's Pelle . . . You don't understand what it costs them . . . Well, they too have the same urge . . . Any little thing is enough to save or lose them. . . . That's what political work is . . . to give them a sense . . ."

When Kim talks to the men and analyses the situation for them, he is absolutely clear and dialectical. But when he is talking like this just to one other person to hear him, it makes one's head spin. Ferreira sees things more simply. "All right, let's give them this sense, let's organise them the way I say."

Kim blows into his moustache. "This isn't an army, you see, they aren't soldiers to whom one can say: this is your duty. You can't talk about duty here, you can't talk about ideals like country, liberty, communism. The men don't want to hear about ideals, anyone can have those, they have ideals on the other side too. You see what happens when that ex-tremist cook begins his sermonising? They shout at him and knock him about. They don't need ideals, myths, to shout 'Long live . . .' They fight and die without shouting anything."

"Why do they fight, then?" asks Ferriera. He knows why he does, everything is perfectly clear to him.

"Well," says Kim, "at this moment the various detachments are climbing silently up towards their positions. To-morrow many of them will be wounded or dead. They know that. What drives them to lead this life, what makes them fight? Well, first, the peasants who live in these mountains, it's easier with them. The Germans burn their villages, take away their cattle. Theirs is a basic human war, one to defend their own country, for the peasants really have a country. So they join up with us, young and old, with their old shot-guns and cartridge pouches; whole villages of them; they're with us as we're defending their country. And defending their country becomes a serious ideal for them, transcends them, as an end in itself; they sacrifice even their homes, even their cattle, to go on fighting. Then there are other peasants for whom 'country' remains something selfish; *their* cattle, *their* homes, *their* crops. And to keep all that they become spies, Fascists . . . there are whole villages which are our enemies. Then there are the workers. The workers have a background of their own, of wages and strikes, work and struggle elbow to elbow. They're a class, the workers are. They know there's something better in life and they fight for that something better. They have a 'country' too, a 'country' still to be conquered, and they're fighting to conquer it. Down in the town there are factories which will be theirs; they can already see the red writing on the walls and the banners flying on the factory chimneys. But there's no sentimentality in them. They understand reality and how to change it. Red Wolf, for instance. D'you see what I mean? Red Wolf! Then there is an intellectual or a student or two, very few of them though, here and there, with ideas in their heads that are often vague or twisted.

Their 'country' consists of words, or at the most of some book. But as they fight they find that those words of theirs no longer have any meaning, and they make new discoveries about men's struggles, and they just fight on without asking themselves questions, until they can find new words and rediscover the old ones, changed now, with unsuspected meanings. Who else is there? Foreign prisoners, who've escaped from concentration camps and joined us; they're fighting for a real proper country, a distant country which they want to get back to and which is theirs just because it is distant. But, after all, is this only a struggle between symbols? Must a man, to kill a German, think not of that German but of something else, with a substitution which is enough to turn his brain? Must everything and everybody become a Chinese shadow-play, a myth?"

Ferriera strokes his blond beard; he doesn't see anything in all this.

"It's not like that," he says.

"No, it's not like that," Kim goes on, "I know that too. It's not like that. Because there's something else, common to all of them. Take Dritto's detachment; petty thieves, *carabinieri*, ex-soldiers, black marketeers, down-and-outs; men on the fringes of society, who got along somehow, with nothing to defend and nothing to lose; either they're defective physically, or they have fixations, or they're fanatics. No revolutionary idea can ever appear there, linked as they are to the millstones grinding them. Or if it does it will be born twisted, the child of rage and humiliation, such as that extremist cook's, whose talk is like the screeches of that trained hawk of his. Why do they fight, then? They have no 'country,' either real or invented. And yet you know there's courage, there's hatred in them too. And that hatred is due to a resentment they have dragged along with them since their childhood, and which may be either lively or dormant. It comes from the squalor of their lives, the filth of their homes, the obscenities they've known ever since babyhood, the strain of having to be bad.

All that has become hatred, an anonymous, aimless, dumb hatred, which finds expression here in firing machine-guns, making prisoners dig their own graves, and in a bitter yearning to get to grips with the enemy. And any little thing, a false step, a momentary impulse, is enough to send them over to the other side, to the Black Brigade, like Pelle, there to shoot with the same resentment, the same hatred, against either side, it doesn't matter which."

Ferriera mutters into his beard: "So you think the spirit of our men . . . and the Black Brigade's . . . the same thing?"

"The same thing, the same thing . . . but, if you see what I mean . . ." Kim has stopped, with a finger pointing as if he were keeping the place in a book, "The same thing but the other way round. Because here we're in the right, there they're in the wrong. Here we're achieving something, there they're just strengthening the rivets. That age-old resentment which weighs down on Dritto's men, on all of us, including you and me, and which finds expression in shooting and killing enemies, the Fascists have that too. But with us nothing is lost, not a gesture, not a shot, though each may be the same as theirs — d'you see what I mean? — they will all serve if not to free us then to free our children, to create a world that is serene, without resentment, a world in which no one has to be bad. The others are on the side of lost gestures, of useless resentment, which are lost and useless even if they should win, because they are not making positive history, they are not helping to free themselves but to repeat and perpetuate resentment and hatred, until in another twenty or a hundred or a thousand years it will begin all over again, the struggle between us and them; and we shall both be fighting with the same anonymous hatred in our eyes, though always, perhaps without knowing it, *we* shall be fighting for redemption, *they* to remain slaves. That is the real meaning of the struggle now, the real, absolute meaning, beyond the various official meanings. An elementary, anonymous urge to vindicate all our humiliations; the worker from his exploitation, the peasant from his ignorance, the petty bourgeois from his inhibitions, the outcast from his corruption. This is what I believe our political work is, to use human misery against itself, for our own redemption, as the Fascists use misery to perpetuate misery and man fighting man."

Only the blue of Ferriera's eyes and the yellow glimmer of his beard can be seen in the dark. He shakes his head. He does not feel this resentment; he is precise as a mechanic and practical as a mountaineer; for him the struggle is a precise machine of which he knows the workings and purpose.

"It seems impossible," he says, "it seems impossible that with all that nonsense in your head you can still be a good commissar and talk clearly to the men."

Kim is not displeased at Ferriera not understanding him; men like Ferriera must be talked to in exact terms; "a, b, c," one must say, things are either definite or they're "balls," for them there are no ambiguous or dark areas. But Kim does not reason that way, and so he believes himself to be superior to Ferriera; but now he would like to be able to think like Ferriera, to see no other reality but Ferriera's.

"Well, I'll say good-bye." They have reached a parting in the path. Now Ferriera will go on to Gamba's detachment and Kim to Baleno's. They have to separate in order to be able to inspect every detachment that night, before the battle.

Nothing else matters. Kim walks on alone, the slim Stengun hanging from his shoulder like a broken walking-stick. Nothing else matters. The tree trunks in the dark take on strange human shapes. Man carries his babyhood fears with him for his whole life long. "Perhaps," thinks Kim, "I'd be frightened, if I wasn't brigade commissar. Not to be frightened any more, that's the final aim of man."

Kim is logical when he is analysing the situation with the detachment commissars, but when he is walking along alone and reasoning with himself things become mysterious and magical again, and life seems full of miracles. Our heads are still full of magic and miracles, thinks Kim. Sometimes he feels he is walking amid a world of symbols, like his namesake, little Kim in the middle of India, in that book of Kipling's which he had so often re-read as a boy.

"Kim . . . Kim . . . Who is Kim . . . ?"

Now that he is walking over the mountains on the night before a battle, has he, he wonders, turned out to be right about life and death, after that gloomy childhood of his as a rich man's son, and his shy adolescence? Well, his thoughts are logical, he can analyse everything with perfect clarity. But no, he's not serene. His parents were serene, those parents from the great middle class which created their own riches. The proletariat is serene for it knows what it wants, so are the peasants who are now doing sentry duty over their own villages. Will Kim ever be serene? One day perhaps, if we all achieve serenity and do not understand so much because we will have understood everything. Now we still give too much weight to things that don't exist.

Here men still have troubled eyes and haggard faces. Kim has become fond of these men, though. That little boy in Dritto's detachment, for instance. What's his name? With that rage eating up his freckly face, even when he laughs . . . He's said to be the brother of a prostitute. Why is he fighting? He doesn't know it's so that he should no longer be the brother of a prostitute. And those Calabrian brothers-in-law. They're fighting so as not to be despised folk from the south any more. And that Carabiniere is fighting so that he won't feel a Carabiniere any more, always at the heels of others like him. Then there's Cousin, the good, gigantic, ruthless Cousin . . . We all have a secret wound which we are fighting to avenge. Even Ferriera? Yes, perhaps even Ferriera; the incapacity of being able to get the world to go as he wants it. Not Red Wolf, though. Because everything that Red Wolf wants is possible.

He must be made to want the right thing, that is political work. And learn that what he wants is right; that too is political work, commissar's work.

Perhaps, one day, thinks Kim, I won't understand these things any more. I'll be serene, and understand men in a completely different way, a juster way, perhaps. Why perhaps? Well, I shan't say "perhaps" any more then, there won't be any more "perhaps" in me. And I'll have Dritto shot. Now I'm too linked to them and all their twists. To Dritto too. I know that Dritto must suffer a lot for always being determined to behave badly. Nothing in the world hurts so much as behaving badly. One day as a child I shut myself up for two days in my room without speaking. I suffered terribly but would not open the door and they had to come and fetch me by ladder through the window. I longed to be consoled and understood. Dritto feels the same. But he knows we'll shoot him. He wants to be shot. That longing gets hold of men sometimes. And Pelle, what is Pelle doing at this moment?

Kim walks on through a larch wood and thinks of Pelle down in the town going round on curfew patrol with the death's head badge on his cap. Pelle must be alone, alone with his anonymous mistaken hatred, alone with his betrayal gnawing at him and making him behave worse than ever to justify it. He'll shoot at the cats in the black-out, even, from rage, and the shots will wake the sleepers nearby, and make them start up in their beds.

Kim thinks of the column of Germans and Fascists who are perhaps at that moment advancing up the valley, towards the dawn which will bring death pouring down on their heads from the crests of the mountains. It is a column of lost gestures. One of the soldiers is waking up at a jolt of the truck and thinking "I love you Kate." In six or seven hours he'll be dead, we'll have killed him; even if he hadn't thought

"I love you Kate," it would have been the same; everything that he does or thinks is lost, cancelled from history.

I on the other hand am walking through a larch wood and every step I take is history. I think "I love you Adriana" and that is history, will have great consequences. I'll behave to-morrow in battle like a man who has thought to-night "I love you Adriana." Perhaps I don't do any great things, but history is made up of little anonymous gestures; I may die to-morrow even before that German, but everything I do before dying and my death too will be little parts of history, and all the thoughts I'm having now will influence my history to-morrow, to-morrow's history of the human race.

Now, instead of escaping into phantasy as I did when I was a child, I should be making a mental study of the details of the attack, the dispositions of weapons and squads. But I like thinking about those men, studying them, making discoveries about them. What will they do "afterwards" for instance? Will they recognise in post-war Italy something made by them? Red Wolf will understand, I think; I wonder what he'll do to put his understanding into practise, how will he use that adventurous ingenious spirit of his when there are no more sudden attacks or escapes to be made? We should all be like Red Wolf. There'll be some, on the other hand, whose anonymous resentment will continue, who will become individualists again, and thus sterile; they'll fall into crime, the great outlet for dumb resentments; they'll forget that history once walked by their side, breathed through their clenched teeth. The ex-Fascists will say: "Oh, the partisans! I told you so! I realised it at once!" And they won't have realised anything, either before or after.

One day Kim will be serene. Everything is clear with him now. Dritto, Pin, the Calabrian brothers-in-law. He knows how to behave towards each of them, without fear or pity. Sometimes when he is walking at night the mists of souls seem to condense around him like the mists in the air; but he is a man who analyses; "a, b, c," he'll say to the commissars; he's a man who dominates situations. "I love you Adriana."

The valley is full of mist, and Kim is walking along a stony path as if he were on a lakeside. The larches appear out of the mist like mooring-poles. *Kim . . . Kim . . . Who is Kim?* He feels like the hero of that novel read in his child-hood; the half-English half-Indian boy who travels across India looking for the river of purification.

Two hours ago he was talking to that liar Dritto, to the prostitute's brother, and now he is reaching the detachment of Baleno, the best in the brigade. There is a squad of Russians with Baleno, ex-prisoners who had escaped from the fortification works on the frontier.

"Who goes there?"

It's the sentry; a Russian.

Kim gives his name.

"Bring news, Commissar?"

It's Aleksjéi, the son of a moujik, an engineering student.

"To-morrow there will be a battle, Aleksjéi."

"Battle? Hundred Fascists *kaput?*"

"I don't know how many *kaput*, Aleksjéi. I don't even know how many alive."

"Salt and tobacco, Commissar."

Salt and tobacco is the Italian phrase which has made most impression on Aleksjéi, he repeats it all the time, like a refrain, a talisman.

"Salt and tobacco, Aleksjéi."

To-morrow there will be a big battle. Kim is serene. "A, b, c," he'll say. Again and again he thinks: "I love you Adriana." That, and that alone, is history.

CHAPTER TEN

IN THE dark morning, without a glimmer of light, Dritto's men are moving silently around the barn, preparing to leave. They wrap blankets round their shoulders; it will be cold up on the boulders of the crest before dawn. As they do so they think not of what will happen to themselves but to this blanket they are taking with them. Will they lose it running away, will it be soaked with their blood as they lie dying, or be taken from them by a Fascist and shown round the town as booty? But what does a blanket matter?

Above them, as if the sound came from above the clouds, they can hear the enemy column on the move; big wheels turning on dusty roads without headlights, the tramp of tired men asking their section leader if they still have far to go. Dritto's men talk in whispers as if the column were passing right behind the walls of the barn.

Now they are munching boiled chestnuts out of their billy-cans; no one knows when they will eat next. The cook will be going into action too, this time; he is ladling out the chestnuts, cursing under his breath, his eyes swollen with sleep, and he does not mention revolution any more. Giglia has also got up and is wandering round among the preparations without finding anything useful to do. Every now and again Mancino pauses to glance at her.

"Hey, Giglia," he says, "it's not safe for you to stay here in the camp alone. One never knows."

"Where d'you expect me to go to, then?" asks Giglia.

"Put on your skirt and go to a village, they won't do anything to a woman. Dritto, tell her she can't stay here alone."

Dritto has not eaten any chestnuts, he is directing the men's preparations almost silently, with his collar up. He does not raise his head or reply at once.

109

"No," he says eventually, "she'd better stay here."

Giglia glances at her husband as if to say, "You see?" Then the men try to get rid of her, saying, "Out of the way," until finally she goes back to sleep.

Pin is also in everybody's way, like a hunting dog watching its master's preparations.

"A battle," he thinks, trying to excite himself, "now there'll be a battle."

"Well," he says to Giacinto, "which shall I take?"

The commissar takes no notice of him. "What?" he says.

"Which rifle shall I take?" asks Pin.

"You?" exclams Giacinto. "You're not coming."

"Yes, I am."

"Out of the way. This isn't a time to take children along. Dritto doesn't want you to come. Out of the way."

Pin is furious, he'll follow behind them unarmed, jeering at their backs till they turn and shoot at him.

"Dritto, Dritto, is it true you don't want me to come?"

Dritto doesn't reply, he is taking little puffs at a cigarette-end, as if he were biting it.

"There," says Pin, "he says it's not true."

Now I'll get a clip on the back of the head, he thinks. But Dritto says nothing.

"Can I go into action, Dritto?" says Pin.

Dritto smokes.

"Dritto says I can come, did you hear, Giacinto?" exclaims Pin.

Now Dritto will say: "Shut up; you stay here."

Instead of which he says nothing. Why?

Pin says, very loudly, "Then I'm coming."

And he goes towards a place where there are still some unallotted weapons, whistling so as to attract attention to himself. He chooses the lightest rifle.

"Then I'll take this," he says, loudly.

"Does it belong to anyone, this one?"

No answer. Pin goes back to where he was before, swinging the rifle to and fro by its strap. He sits down on the ground, right in front of Dritto, and begins testing the bolt, the firing-pin, the trigger, crooning: "I have a rifle! I have a rifle!"

Someone shouts: "Quiet! Are you mad?"

The men are getting into single file, squad by squad, group by group; the ammunition bearers arrange their shifts.

"You understand, then," says Dritto, "the detachment will take up position between the pilon on Mount Pellegrino and the second gorge. Cousin will take over command. New orders when we arrive up there."

Now all the men's eyes are on him, sleepy turgid eyes, crossed by locks of hair.

"What about you?" they ask.

Dritto's lowered lids are covered with a slight discharge. "I'm ill," he says, "I can't come."

There, now everything can just take its course. The men say nothing. "I'm a finished man," thinks Dritto. Now every-thing can take its course. It's terrible, though, that the men say nothing, make no protest; that means they've already condemned him, are pleased at his refusing this last test. Perhaps they expected it. And yet they cannot understand what it is that makes him do this; neither does he, Dritto, himself. But now everything can take its course, there is nothing for him to do but let himself drift.

Pin, on the other hand, understands everything; he is watching attentively, his tongue between his teeth, his eyes alight. There lies the woman, with that warm breast of hers under the man's shirt, half-buried in the hay. It's hot in the hay and she keeps on turning over. Once at night she got up when everyone was asleep, took off her trousers and got back naked between the blankets. Pin saw her. Yes, astounding things will be happening in the barn while the battle rages in the valley, things a hundred times more exciting. That must be why Dritto is allowing Pin to go into action. Pin has dropped the rifle at his feet and is following every movement with his eyes, very attentively. The men continue getting into line; no one tells Pin to do so.

At that moment the hawk begins screeching from the rafters in the roof, flapping its clipped wings as if in sudden desperation.

"Babeuf! I must feed Babeuf!" cries Mancino, and he runs to fetch the sack of entrails. Then the men turn against him and the bird, as if wanting to deflect all their rancour on to something positive.

"Hell take you and your hawk! Filthy bird of ill omen! Some disaster happens every time it opens its mouth! Twist its neck! Twist its neck!"

Mancino faces them with the hawk perched by the claws on his shoulder, feeding it bits of meat and looking at his comrades with hatred. "The hawk's mine, it's nothing to do with you, and I'll take it into action with me if I want to, d'you get that?"

"Twist its neck!" cries Long Zena. "This isn't the time to think of hawks! Twist its neck or we will!"

He tries to grab it, and gets a bite on the back of his hand that draws blood. The hawk's feathers are standing on end, it is spreading its wings and screeching ceaselessly, rolling its yellow eyes.

"There! There! I'm glad!" cries the cook. The men are all standing round him, their beards bristling with rage, their fists raised.

"Shut it up! Shut it up! It brings bad luck! It'll call the Germans down on us!"

Long Zena sucks the blood on his wounded hand.

"Kill it!" he shouts.

Duke, who is carrying the machine-gun, takes a pistol from his belt.

"I'll shoot it! I'll shoot it!" he grunts.

The hawk, rather than showing any sign of quietening down, is becoming more and more frenzied.

"All right," Mancino suddenly decides. "All right. Just see what I'm going to do. You wanted it."

He has taken the hawk by the neck in both his hands and is now pulling, holding the head between his knees, towards the ground. The men are all silent.

"There. Now you're satisfied. You're all satisfied, now. There."

The hawk is not moving any more, its clipped wings are hanging open, its stiff feathers drooping. Mancino flings it on to a bush, and Babeuf remains hanging there by its wings, with its head down. It gives a last quiver, then dies.

"Into line. All into line and let's go," calls Cousin. "Machine-gunners ahead, ammunition bearers behind. Riflemen last. Let's go."

Pin is standing to one side. He does not get into line. Dritto turns and enters the barn. In silence the men start off along the track leading up into the mountains. Last is Mancino in his sailor's jersey with the bird-droppings all over his shoulders.

Inside the barn the darkness smells of hay. The woman and the man are asleep in opposite corners, wrapped in their blankets. Neither moves. Pin could swear, though, that neither will close an eye again till daybreak. He lies down also, with his eyes open. He will look and listen, and not close an eye either. The two are not even scratching themselves. They are breathing deeply. Yet they are awake, Pin knows that; and gradually he falls asleep.

It is daylight outside when he wakes up. Pin is all alone among trampled straw. Gradually he remembers everything. It's the day of the battle! Why is there no sound of firing? It's the day when the commander will have the cook's wife! Pin gets up and goes out. The sky is so blue it's almost frightening, and so many birds singing they're almost frightening too.

The kitchen has been set up among the ruins of an old hut. Giglia is inside. She is fanning a small fire under a canful of chestnuts; she looks pale, with dull eyes.

"Pin! D'you want some chestnuts?" she calls with that false motherly air of hers as if she were trying to keep him sweet.

Pin hates women putting on maternal airs; he knows it's all a trick and that they, like his sister, really hate him and are just afraid of him. He hates her.

Has "it" happened? And where is Dritto? He decides to ask her.

"Well; done everything?" he asks.

"What?" exclaims Giglia.

Pin does not reply; he glances at her from half-closed eyes, wrinkling his nose.

"I've just got up," says Giglia, looking angelic.

She understands — thinks Pin — the cow. She's understood.

And yet he has a feeling that nothing definite has happened yet; the woman is looking tense and holding her breath.

Dritto arrives. He's been washing; around his neck is a faded coloured towel. His face looks older, covered with lines and shadows.

"They're not firing yet," he says.

"Hell, Dritto," exclaims Pin. "Have they all fallen asleep?"

Dritto doesn't smile; he is sucking his teeth.

"Has the whole brigade fallen asleep on the crest, d'you think?" says Pin. "And the Germans getting here on tiptoe? *Raus! Raus!* We turn round and there they are."

Pin points behind Dritto, who turns around. Then he is annoyed with himself for turning, and shrugs his shoulders. He sits down by the fire.

"I'm ill," he says.

"D'you want some chestnuts?" asks Giglia.

Dritto spits into the cinders.

"My stomach's burning," he says.

"Just drink the juice."

"My stomach's burning."

Then he thinks it over. "All right. Give me some," he says.

He brings the lip of the dirty billy-can to his lips and drinks. Then he puts it down.

"Good. I'm eating," says Pin.

And he begins to suck at the mess of hot chestnuts.

Dritto raises his eyes towards Giglia. His eyelids have long hard lashes on top; the ones underneath are bare.

"Dritto," says the woman.

"Mmm."

"Why didn't you go?"

Pin keeps his face inside the tin and looks at them from above the brim.

"Go where?"

"Into action, of course."

"How can I go anywhere, when I don't know where I am myself!"

"What's wrong, Dritto?"

"What's wrong? I know what's wrong! They've got it in for me at brigade, they've been playing cat and mouse with me for some time. It's always: hey, Dritto we'll talk about this afterwards, now take care, Dritto, think it over, Dritto, be careful . . . Devil take them. I can't stand it any more. If they've something to say to me let them say it. I want to do what I like a bit."

Giglia is sitting a little above him. She gives him a long look, breathing hard through her nostrils.

"I feel I want to do what I like a bit," Dritto tells her, his eyes yellow. He puts a hand on her knee.

Pin is sucking noisily at the empty tin.

"Dritto, suppose they really get at you?"

Dritto moves nearer her, now he is crouching at her feet.

"I don't mind dying," he says. But his lips are trembling, the lips of a sick boy. "I don't mind dying. But first I'd like . . . First . . ."

His head is turned up and he is looking at Giglia above him.

Pin throws the empty tin on to the ground, with the spoon inside. Dlin! goes the spoon.

Dritto now turns his head towards him, and looks at him, gnawing his lips.

"Eh!" says Pin.

Dritto gives a start.

"They're not firing," he says.

"They're not firing," says Pin.

Dritto gets up, and walks round a little, nervously.

"Go and fetch some water, Pin."

"Right away," says Pin, and bends down to do up his boots.

"You're pale, Giglia," says Dritto. He is standing behind her, with his knees touching her back.

"Perhaps I'm ill too," breathes Giglia.

Pin breaks out into one of his monotonous songs in an endless crescendo: "She's pale! . . . She's pale! . . . She's pale! . . . She's pale! . . ."

The man has put his hands on her cheeks and turned her face up. "Ill like me . . . ? Say, ill like me . . . ?"

"She's pale! . . . She's pale! . . . She's pale! . . ." sings Pin.

Dritto turns on him with a furious face.

"What about the water?"

"Wait a sec . . ." says Pin. "I'll just do the other up." And he goes on fiddling with his boots.

"I don't know how you're ill . . ." says Giglia. "How are you ill?"

Dritto says in a low voice, "So ill I can't stand it any more, can't stand it any more."

Now, still from behind her, he has taken her by the shoulders and is holding his hands under her arm-pits.

"She's pale! . . . She's pale! . . ."

"Pin!"

"Right. I'm off now. Give me the flask."

Then he stops, with a hand to his ear. Dritto also stops, and looks out into the emptiness.

"They're not firing," he says.

"Neh? They're not firing at all . . ." says Pin.

They both stand there silently.

"Pin!"

"I'm going!"

Pin leaves, dangling the flask and whistling the tune he has been singing. There'll be a lot to amuse him to-day. Pin will be quite pitiless; Dritto does not frighten him now he's not in command any more; he'll never command anything again, now he's refused to go into action. Pin's whistling can no longer be heard from the kitchen. He stops, turns round and tiptoes back. No, they're still where they were. Dritto's hands are now under her hair, at the nape of her neck, and she is making cat-like movements as if to avoid them. They turn at once, with a start, sensing his presence.

"Well?" exclaims Dritto.

"I came to fetch the other flask," says Pin. "The straw's undone on this one."

Dritto passes a hand over his forehead. "Here you are."

The woman gets up and goes and sits near the sack of potatoes.

"Well. Let's peel some potatoes; at least we'll be doing something."

She lays an empty sack on the ground and puts potatoes and a couple of knives on it.

"Take a knife, Dritto, here are the potatoes," she says.

Pin thinks her silly and hypocritical.

Dritto is still passing a hand over his forehead. "They're not firing yet," he says, "I wonder what's happening?"

Pin goes out again; this time he really will go and fetch water. They'll have to be given time, otherwise nothing will ever happen. Near the spring is a bushful of blackberries. Pin settles down to picking and eating them. He likes blackberries, but finds they give him no pleasure now; although he fills his mouth with them he can't taste any flavour. There; now he's eaten enough, he can return. But perhaps it's still too soon; better if he can get something else over first. He crouches down among the bushes. It makes him feel good to force himself and meanwhile think of Dritto and Giglia chasing each other round the ruined hut, or of those prisoners being led out into the darkness and made to kneel down in the graves they've dug themselves, with chattering teeth; evil incomprehensible things, as strangely fascinating to him as his own excrement.

He wipes himself with leaves. He's ready, off he goes.

In the kitchen the potatoes are spilled all over the floor. Giglia is in a corner beyond the sacks and cooking-pots, with a knife in her hand. Her man's shirt is open; Dritto is also standing on the other side of the sacks, and is threatening her with his knife. Yes, they are chasing each other, perhaps they'll wound each other next!

Instead of which, he is laughing; they are both laughing; it's all a game. It's not nice laughter, and the joke seems to hurt them, but they are laughing.

Pin puts down the flask. "The water," he says loudly.

They leave their knives now and come to drink. Dritto takes the flask and gives it to Giglia. Giglia grasps it and drinks, while Dritto looks at her lips.

He says, "They're not firing yet."

Then he turns towards Pin. "They're not firing yet," he repeats. "What on earth's happening down there?"

Pin is pleased at being asked a question like that, as between equals.

"What d'you think can be happening?" he asks.

Dritto drinks in great gulps, empties the flask down his throat, and never seems to be going to stop. He dries his mouth. "There, Giglia, if you want any more. Drink up if you're thirsty, then we'll send for another."

"If you want me to," says Pin sourly, "I'll bring you a pailful."

They both look at each other and laugh. But Pin realises they're not laughing at what he said; it's a laugh between the two of them, secret, without any reason.

"If you like," says Pin, "I'll bring you enough to bathe in."

They go on looking at each other and laughing.

"To bathe in," repeats the man, and it's difficult now to tell if he's laughing or if his teeth are chattering. "To bathe in, Giglia, to bathe in."

He has taken her by the shoulders. Then suddenly his face darkens and he drops his hands. "Down there," he says, "look down there."

Hanging on a bush, a few yards away, is the dead hawk, dangling on its wings.

"Away with it. Away with the filthy thing," he says, "I don't want to see it any more!"

He takes it up by one of its wings and flings it far into the alpenroses; Babeuf flies off as perhaps he never did in his life. Giglia puts a hand on Dritto's arm. "No, poor Babeuf!"

"Away with it," Dritto is pale with anger. "I don't want to see it any more! Go and bury it, Pin! Pin, go and bury it. Take the spade and bury it, Pin!"

Pin looks at the dead bird in the alpenroses; suppose it gets up, dead though it is, and bites him right between the eyes?

"No, I won't," he says.

Dritto's nostrils quiver; he puts a hand on his pistol.

"Take the spade, Pin, and get going."

Pin takes the hawk up by a leg; the claws are curved, and hard as nails. He sets off with the spade on his shoulders, carrying the dead bird with its head dangling down. Through the alpenroses and a patch of woodland and he's out in the meadows. Under those meadows rising in gradual slopes up towards the mountains all the dead are buried, with eyes full of earth, dead enemies and dead comrades. And now the hawk as well.

Pin walks over the meadows in curious twists and turns. He doesn't want, when he digs a grave for the bird, to uncover a human face with his spade. He doesn't want to disturb the dead at all, he's afraid of them. And yet it would be fine to dig up a dead body, a dead man with his teeth bare and his eyes empty.

Now Pin can only see mountains around him, and huge valleys with invisible depths, and high rocky slopes black with woods, then mountains again, row after row of them, into the infinite distance. He is alone on the earth. Under the earth are the dead. Beyond the woods and slopes there are other human beings, rubbing themselves against each other, or shooting to kill. At his feet lies the dead hawk. Huge clouds are flying above him in the windswept sky. Pin begins digging out a grave for the dead bird. A small grave is enough; a hawk is not a man. Pin takes it up; its eyes are shut, with bare, almost human-looking lids. If he tried to open one, he would see the round yellow eye beneath. He feels an impulse to fling the hawk into the great empty space above the valley and see its wings open, then watch it rise in flight, circle above his head and fly off towards a distant peak. And then he would follow it as they do in fairy stories, walking over mountains and plains until he reached an enchanted village in which all the inhabitants were good. But instead Pin now puts the hawk down into the grave and rakes earth on it with the tip of the spade.

At that moment an explosion, like a thunderbolt fills the

valley; shots, bursts, deep bangs, all increased by echoes. The
battle! Pin jumps back in terror. Terrible noises lacerate the
air very near him, he can't tell where. Soon bullets will be
falling right on top of him. Soon the Germans will be appear-
ing on the rocky slopes, bristling with machine-guns, and be
on him.

"Dritto!"

Pin runs away. He's left the spade sticking in the earth
of the grave. He runs with the lacerating noises exploding
all round him.

"Dritto! Giglia!"

There; now he's in the wood. Machine-gun fire, grenades,
mortars; the battle has suddenly started out of its sleep and
it's impossible to tell where it is; perhaps only a few yards
from him; perhaps he'll see machine-guns firing at him at the
turn of this path, and dead men lying among the bushes.

"Help! Dritto! Giglia!"

He is out among the alpenroses now. Under the open
sky the shooting is more frightening than ever.

"Dritto! Giglia!"

No one in the kitchen. They've escaped! Left him alone!

"Dritto! They're firing! They're firing!"

Pin runs haphazardly among the banks of alpenroses,
sobbing. There, in the bushes, is a blanket, a blanket wrapped
round a moving human body; one body . . . no, two bodies
. . . two pairs of legs are showing . . . twined together.

"The battle! Dritto! They're firing! The battle!"

CHAPTER ELEVEN

THE BRIGADE has reached the Pass of the Half-Moon after
endless hours of marching. There is a cold night wind blowing
which freezes the sweat into the bones; the men are too tired

to sleep and the commanders order a short halt behind some
rocky boulders. In the dim cloudy darkness the pass looks like
a concave bowl with its rims wreathed in mist, from which rise
the top of two rocky heights. Beyond it lie free plains and
valleys, fresh areas not yet occupied by the enemy. The men
have not rested since they set off for the battle, yet they show
no sign of any of those dangerous collapses which are apt to
come suddenly after long strain; the stimulant of battle has
not worn off yet.

The battle has been a bloody one and ended in retreat;
but it was not lost. The Germans, passing through a defile,
had suddenly found the heights around pullulating with
shouting men and blazing with firearms; many of them were
rolled into the sides of the track, one or two lorries began
belching fire and smoke like furnaces and were soon reduced
to nothing but black scrap-iron. Reinforcements then came
up, but there was little they could do except wipe out a few
partisans who had stayed on the road against orders or been
cut off in the confusion. For the partisan commanders had
been warned in time of the new motorised column approach-
ing, and to avoid being surrounded had withdrawn their men
up the mountain paths. The Germans, however, are not
people to be put off by a reverse, and Ferriera has decided that
the entire brigade is to evacuate the area, which could now
become a trap, and move on into other valleys where there
were no partisans yet and which could be more easily de-
fended. Now the blackness of the night was left behind as
the retreating men wound up, silent and orderly, along a mule
path leading to the pass; in the rear came a line of mules
carrying rations and ammunition, and the wounded from the
battle.

Dritto's men are now chattering with cold behind the
boulders; their heads and shoulders are wrapped in blankets,
like burnouses. The detachment has had one casualty — the
commissar, Giacinto the tinker. He had been hit by a burst

of German fire and his body lay in a meadow below, rid now
of all his dreams of vagabondage and of all his lice too, which
no insect powder had ever done. There was also one man
slightly wounded in a hand, Count, one of the Calabrian
brothers-in-law.

They have now been joined by Dritto, whose yellow face
and blanket round his shoulders make him look really ill.
Silent, his nostrils quivering, he watches the men one by one.
Every now and again he seems on the point of giving some
order, then says nothing. The men have not said a word to
him yet. If he gave an order, or any of them talked to him,
the rest would certainly turn on him, and violent words would
fly. But this is not the moment for a show-down; both he and
the men realise that by tacit consent, so he avoids giving
orders and the men avoid any occasion for them. The detachment has been marching with discipline, and there has been
no dispersion or quarrel about shifts; one could never have
told it was leaderless. But Dritto is still in fact their leader, he
only has to glance at a man to make him straighten up; yes,
he has a magnificent leader's temperament, Dritto.

Pin, wrapped up to the eyes in a woollen scarf, is looking
at Dritto and Giglia, and from them to Mancino. Their faces
seem quite normal, perhaps rather drawn from cold and ex-
haustion; there is nothing on either of their faces to show what
they'd been doing the morning before.

Other detachments pass which are to halt farther on or
continue their march.

"Gian! Gian!"

In a squad which has halted nearby, Pin suddenly recognises his old friend from the tavern, Gian the Driver, dressed
as a partisan and armed from head to foot. At first he does
not realise who is calling him, then he is just as surprised
himself: "Oh . . . Pin!"

They greet each other with rather cautious warmth, as
people do who are not used to exchanging compliments. Gian

looks a different man; he has only been with the partisans a week, and his eyes have already lost that look of a cave-dwelling animal, due to smoke and alcohol, which those of the men in the tavern have. He is in Spada's detachment.

"When I joined the brigade Kim wanted to put me in your detachment . . ." says Gian. Pin thinks: He doesn't realise what that means, perhaps the man from the committee that night at the tavern reported badly on all of them.

"Hell, Gian, I wish we were together!" says Pin. "Why didn't they put you with us?"

"They told me it was pointless; your detachment is to be broken up soon!"

There, thinks Pin, he's only just arrived and knows all the latest news about us. Pin, on the other hand, knows nothing about things down in the town. "Gian!" he says, "what's the news from Long Alley? And the tavern?"

Gian looks at him sourly: "Haven't you heard?" he asks.

"No," says Pin, "what is it? Has the Bersagliera had a child?"

Gian spits. "I don't want to hear another word about those people," he says. "I'm ashamed of being born among them. For years I've been fed up to the eyes with them and the tavern, the stink in the Alley . . . And yet I stayed there . . . Now I've been forced to run away I can almost thank the swine who informed on me. . . ."

"Frenchy Michel?" asks Pin.

"Michel was one. But he's not the one who did most. He plays a double game, Michel does, with the Black Brigade and with the *Gap;* he hasn't properly decided yet which side to be on. . . ."

"And the others . . . ?"

"There was a round-up. They were all taken. We'd only just decided to form a *Gap* . . . Giraffe was shot . . . The others taken to Germany . . . The Alley's almost emptied . . . A bomb from an aeroplane fell near the bakery; everyone has either evacuated or is living in the tunnel . . . It's another life here; I feel as if I were back in Croatia, only now, thank God, I'm on the other side. . . ."

"In Croatia, Gian, what on earth did you find in Croatia, a mistress? And my sister, tell me, has she been evacuated too?"

Gian strokes his newly growing beard: "Your sister," he says, "has made others evacuate, the cow."

"Explain yourself," says Pin, acting the buffoon. "You're offending me, you know."

"Idiot! Your sister is in the S.S., and wears silk dresses and goes driving round with officers! When the Germans came to the Alley, she was the one who led them from house to house, arm-in-arm with a German captain!"

"A captain, Gian! She *has* got on in the world!"

"Are you talking about women informers?" This is said by Cousin, who is thrusting his big face with its flattened nose and its sprouting moustaches towards them.

"Yes, that bitch of a sister of mine," says Pin. "She's been a spy and sneak ever since she was a child. This was to be expected."

"It was to be expected," says Cousin, looking into the distance with that disconsolate expression of his, from under the woollen cap.

"It was to be expected of Frenchy Michel too," says Gian, "but he's not really bad, Michel isn't, he's just a rascal."

"And Pelle, d'you know the new one in the Black Brigade, Pelle?"

"Pelle!" exclaims Gian the Driver. "He's the worst of the lot."

"He *was* the worst," says a voice behind them. They turn round; it's Red Wolf arriving, hung all over with weapons and machine-gun belts captured from the Germans. They greet him warmly; everyone is pleased to see Red Wolf again.

"Why, what's happened to Pelle? How did it go?"

Red Wolf says, "The *Gap* organised it all," and he begins telling them what happened.

Pelle used sometimes to go and sleep at his own home, and not in barracks. He lived by himself in the attic of a tenement block, where he kept the whole armoury of weapons which he'd managed to lay hands on, for if he'd taken them to barracks he'd have had to share them with his companions. One night Pelle was on his way home, armed as always. A man was following him, dressed in civilian clothes and wearing a raincoat. Whenever Pelle saw someone he didn't like the look of, he soon asked for their papers. He stopped, but did not turn round. The other had stopped too, with his hands in his pockets. Pelle felt himself covered by a firearm. "Better pretend not to notice," he thought, and went on walking. On the other pavement there was another man he'd never seen before, also in a raincoat, walking along with his hands in his pockets. Pelle turned and the pair turned too. "I must get home as quickly as possible," he thought. "As soon as I reach the street door I'll jump inside and begin firing from behind the doorposts to keep them off." But beyond the street door, on the pavement, was another man in a raincoat, coming towards him. "Better let him pass," thought Pelle. He stopped and the men in the raincoats stopped too, all three of them. The only thing to do was reach the street door as soon as possible. In the entrance, back against the stair rails, were another two men in raincoats, standing there motionless with their hands in their pockets. Pelle had already entered. "Now they've got me in a trap," he thought. "Now they'll say: 'Hands up!' " But they did not seem to be looking at him. "If they still follow me," he thought, "I'll turn on the stairs and fire down between the rails." When he reached the second flight he looked down. They were following; Pelle was still covered by the invisible weapons in the pockets of their raincoats. Another landing; Pelle frowned down. On each flight of stairs below him was a man coming up. Pelle went on climbing, keeping very close to the wall, but at whatever point of the stairs he'd reached, there was always a man of the *Gap*, one or two or three or four flights below him, coming up close to the wall, and keeping him covered. Six floors, seven floors. The well of the staircase in the dim light of the black-out looked like a series of mirrors, with a man in a raincoat repeated numberless times on every flight, spiralling slowly up towards him. "If they don't fire at me before I reach the attic," thought Pelle, "I'm safe; I'll barricade myself inside and I've got enough weapons and grenades there to resist till the Black Brigade arrives." Now he had reached the last floor under the roof. Pelle ran up the last flight, opened his front-door, entered and banged it to behind him. "I'm safe," he thought. But on the roof, through the windows of the attic, he saw a man in a raincoat aiming a pistol at him. Pelle raised his hands. The door opened behind him. From the stair rails on the landings all the men in raincoats were aiming pistols at him. Then one of them, no one knows who, fired.

The men halted at the pass are all standing round Red Wolf, following the story breathlessly. Red Wolf sometimes exaggerates a little in his stories, but he tells them very well.

One of them says: "What about you, Red Wolf, which of these men were you?"

Red Wolf smiles, and raises his peaked cap on his shaven skull. "The one on the roof," he says.

He then describes all the weapons Pelle had collected up there; stens, tommy-guns, hand-grenades, pistols of every make and calibre. There was even a mortar, says Red Wolf.

"Look," he says, and shows them a pistol and some special hand grenades. "This is all I took, the *Gap* have less weapons than we have, and need them."

Pin suddenly remembers his pistol. If Pelle knew the place and went and fetched it, it must have been among those; and now he, Pin, had a right to it, it was his, and no one could take it from him!

"Red Wolf, listen, Red Wolf?" he says, pulling him by the jacket. "Was there a P.38 among Pelle's pistols?"

"A P.38?" replies the other. "No, there wasn't a P.38. He had every type in the collection, but not a P.38." And he goes on describing the variety and rarity of the weapons collected by the maniac Pelle.

"Are you quite sure there wasn't a P.38?" asks Pin. "Could someone from the *Gap* have taken it?"

"No, no, d'you think I wouldn't have noticed a P.38? We went through them all together."

Then the pistol must still be buried under the spiders' nests, thinks Pin; it's still mine, Pelle didn't know the place, no one knows that magic place but me. This reassures him greatly. Whatever happens, there are still the spiders' nests and the buried pistol.

It is nearly dawn. The brigade still has many hours of marching in front of it, but the leaders consider that lines of men filing along open paths after sunrise would give away their new positions, and decide to wait until the following night before continuing their march in complete secrecy.

This is a frontier area, where for many years the Fascists had been playing at preparing a war which in the end they entered completely unprepared; and the mountains are scattered with a variety of long low military buildings. Ferriera now sends orders for the detachments to scatter round these huts to sleep and keep hidden for the whole of next day, till it is dark or misty enough to start marching again.

Places are assigned to the various units; Dritto's detachment is allotted a small isolated building made of cement, with rings in the walls; it must have been a stable. The men stretch themselves out on a few bits of rotten straw on the floor and close their tired eyes, filled with scenes of battle.

In the morning they find it a nuisance having to stay cooped up in there, and only being able to go out one by one to make water behind a wall; but at least they can rest. They are not allowed to sing, or make any smoke from cooking; down at the bottom of the valley there are villages full of spies, with binoculars trained and ears stretched for any sound. The men have to go and cook in shifts at a military kitchen with an underground flue which comes out some way off.

Pin does not know what to do with himself; he has sat down in a patch of sun at the door and taken off his broken boots and now completely heelless socks. He looks at his feet in the sun, rubs his blisters, and takes the dirt from between his toes. Then he searches for lice; a daily round-up is necessary if he is not to end up like Giacinto, poor old Giacinto. But what is the use of catching lice if one's going to die one day, like Giacinto? Perhaps the reason that Giacinto didn't rid himself of them was that he knew he was going to die. Pin is sad. The first time he caught lice in a shirt was with Pietromagro in prison. Pin wishes he were reopening the cobbler's in the Alley with Pietromagro. But it must be deserted now, the Alley, with everyone run away or taken prisoner or killed, and only that bitch of a sister of his left going round with captains. Pin feels that soon he will find himself abandoned all alone in an unknown world, without any idea where to go. The men of the detachment are an ambiguous stand-offish lot, like the men of the tavern, though much more fascinating and incomprehensible, with that lust to kill in their eyes, and that bestial coupling in the alpenroses. The only one he feels at home with is Cousin, but he's not here now; in the morning on waking up Pin found he had gone, with his woollen cap and his tommy-gun, off on one of his mysterious expeditions. And now the detachment will be broken up, too. Kim and Gian the Driver had said so. The others know nothing about this so far. Pin turns to them as they lie crowded up against each other on the scanty straw on the cement floor.

"God, if I didn't come and give you news, you wouldn't even know you were born."

"What's up now? Spit it out," they say.

"The detachment is to be broken up," he says, "as soon as we get to the new area."

"Get on with you. Who said so?"

"Kim. I swear."

Dritto shows no sign of having heard. He knows what this means.

"Don't talk balls, Pin. Where can they send us?"

They begin to discuss the detachments to which the various men could be assigned, and which they would prefer to go to.

"Don't you know they're going to make a special detachment for each, though?" says Pin. "They'll make all of you commanders. Long Zena they'll make commander of the chair-borne partisans. Sure, a detachment of partisans who go into action sitting down. There are soldiers mounted on horses, aren't there? Now they'll have partisans mounted on rocking-chairs!"

"Wait till I've finished reading," says Long Zena, holding a finger in his *Super-Thriller* to keep the place. "Then I'll answer you. I'm just on the point of guessing the murderer."

"The murderer of the bull?" asks Pin.

Long Zena can no longer follow either his book or the conversation.

"What bull?"

Pin breaks out into one of his high-pitched laughs; Long Zena has fallen into his trap. "The bull you got the lips from! Bull's-lips! Bull's-lips!"

Long Zena leans over on one of his huge hands to get up, still keeping his place, and waves the other about in an attempt to grab Pin; then he realises it's not worth the effort and begins reading again.

The men all laugh at Pin's jokes; they are enjoying themselves; when Pin starts making fun of people he goes right through the lot of them.

Pin, gay and excited, laughs till the tears come into his

eyes; he's in his element, now, right among the grown-ups, people who are enemies and friends at the same time, whom he can laugh at till he has vented his hatred for them. He feels ruthless; he'll hurt them without any pity.

Giglia laughs too, but Pin knows that it's a forced laugh; she is frightened. Pin glances at her now and again; she does not lower her eyes, but the smile is trembling on her lips; you wait, thinks Pin, you won't be laughing long.

"Carabiniere!" exclaims Pin. At every new name he brings in, the men give subdued grins, enjoying in anticipation what Pin will come out with.

"Carabiniere will be given a special detachment . . ." begins Pin.

"To keep order with," says Carabiniere, defensively.

"No, my lad, to arrest parents with!"

Every time Carabiniere is reminded of that business of the conscript's parents, it makes him furious.

"It's not true! I never arrested any of their parents!"

Pin's voice is full of subdued, concentrated irony; the men are listening with approval, backing him up. "Now don't get angry, lad, don't get angry. A detachment to arrest parents with . . . You're so good at arresting parents!"

Carabiniere is getting more and more furious; then suddenly he thinks it might be better to let Pin have his say, till he tires and passes on to someone else.

"Now we'll go on to . . ." Pin swivels his eyes round, then stops with his face set in one of those smiles which bare his gums and cover his eyes with freckles. The men have already guessed who he is referring to, and hold back their laughter. Duke seems almost hypnotised by Pin's grin, his moustache standing straight up and his cheeks are drawn.

". . . there'll be a special detachment for Duke too . . . to gut rabbits. God, you boast so much, Duke, and I've never seen you do anything more than twist chickens' necks and skin rabbits!"

Duke puts a hand on his Austrian pistol and looks as if he's going to gore him with his fur cap. "I'll cccut *your* ggguts out!" he shouts.

Then Mancino makes a false move. He says: "And what shall we put Pin in charge of?"

Pin looks at Mancino as if noticing him for the first time. "Oh, Mancino, you're back, are you . . . ? You've been away from home so long . . . Lots of exciting things have happened while you were away . . ."

He turns round slowly; Dritto is in a corner, looking serious; Giglia is near the door with that hypocritical smile of hers always on her lips.

"Guess what detachment you'll be in charge of, Mancino . . ."

Mancino gives his sour laugh and tries to forestall him: "A cooking-pot detachment . . ." he says, and doubles up with laughter, as if he had made the wittiest joke in the world.

Pin shakes his head, with a serious face. Mancino blinks . . . "a hawk detachment . . ." he says, and tries to laugh again, but only makes a strange sound in his throat.

Pin shakes his head again.

". . . a naval detachment . . ." says Mancino, and now his mouth has not opened, and there are tears in his eyes.

Pin now puts on a clownish hypocritical expression, and says slowly and unctuously: "Well, your detachment won't be so very different from others. Except that it'll only be able to move about in the open, along wide roads, and in places where there's nothing growing higher than bushes."

Mancino begins laughing again, first silently then louder and louder; he has not yet realised what Pin is getting at, but is laughing all the same. The men are now hanging on Pin's lips, some of them have already understood and are grinning.

"It'll be able to go anywhere, except in the woods . . . except where there are branches . . . where there are branches . . ."

"Woods . . . Ha, ha, ha . . . Branches," laughs Mancino. "Why though . . . ?"

"It would get stuck . . . your detachment would . . . get stuck by the horns!"

The others burst into roars of laughter. The cooks gets up, looking sour, his mouth contracted. The laughter drops a little. The cook looks round, then begins laughing himself again, with swollen eyes and twisted mouth, a forced, sullen laugh, and clapping his hands on his knees and pointing to Pin as if to say: "That's a good one . . ."

"Pin . . . take a look at him . . ." he says, grinning falsely now. "Pin . . . we'll give him the lavatory detachment, that's what we'll give him . . ."

Dritto has now got up too.

He takes a step or two towards them. "Stop all this nonsense," he says sharply. "Don't you realise you mustn't make any noise?"

It is the first time since the battle that he has given an order. And he gives it on the excuse that they are not supposed to make any noise, instead of saying: "Stop all this nonsense because I don't like it."

The men give him sour looks; he is no longer their commander, this man.

Giglia's voice is now heard: "Pin, why don't you sing us a song, instead . . . Sing us the one . . ."

"The lavatory detachment . . ." croaks Mancino. "With a po on your head . . . Ha, ha, ha . . . Pin with a po on his head, imagine it. . . ."

"What would you like me to sing you, Giglia?" says Pin. "The same one as . . . ?"

"Shut up," says Dritto. "Don't you know the orders? Don't you know we're in a danger zone?"

"Sing us that song . . ." says Giglia. "The one you do so well . . . How does it go? *Oili, Oilà* . . ."

"With a po on his head," the cook is still laughing and

clapping his knees, though there are tears of rage at the corners of his eyes. "And an enema-tube as a gun . . . A burst of enema-tubes, you'll give, Pin . . ."

"*Oili, Oilà,* Giglia, are you sure . . . ?" says Pin. "I've never heard of any songs that go '*Oili, Oilà*', there aren't any . . ."

"Bursts of enema-tubes . . . Look at him . . . Pin," croaks the cook.

"*Oili, Oilà,*" Pin begins improvising. "The husband goes to war, oilir oilor, and leaves his wife at home, oilim oilom!"

"Pin is a little pimp, oilir oilimp!" shouts Mancino, trying to drown Pin's voice.

Dritto sees that for the first time no one is obeying him. He grabs Pin's arm and begins twisting it: "Shut up! Shut up! D'you understand?"

Pin feels the pain but goes on singing: "Oiler, oiler, the wife and the commander, oili oiloo, what will he do?"

Dritto is now twisting both Pin's arms, feeling the little bones under his fingers; he'll break them in a second, if he goes on. "Shut up, you little bastard, shut up!"

Pin's eyes are full of tears; he is biting his lips: "Oili oilo, to the bushes they go, oili oilogs, like a pair of dogs!"

Dritto drops one of Pin's arms and puts a hand over his mouth. It is a foolish, dangerous thing to do. Pin sinks his teeth into a finger and bites with all his might. Dritto gives a lacerating scream. Pin drops the finger and looks round. They all have their eyes on him, these incomprehensible swine of grown-ups; Dritto is sucking his bleeding finger, Mancino is laughing hysterically, Giglia is looking ashen, and all the others are following the scene breathlessly with glittering eyes.

"Swine!" shouts Pin, breaking into sobs. "Bastards! Bitches!"

The only thing for him now is to escape. Get right away. He must be alone. Pin runs outside.

Dritto is shouting after him: "No one is to leave the

camp! Come back, Pin, come back!" and makes as if to run after him.

But at the door he bumps into two armed men.

"Dritto, we were looking for you."

Dritto recognises them. They are two runners from brigade headquarters.

"Kim and Ferriera want to see you. To report. Come with us."

Dritto becomes impassive again. "Let's go," he says, and picks up his tommy-gun.

"Unarmed, they said," the men explain.

Dritto does not flicker an eyelid; he takes the strap off his shoulder.

"Let's go," he says.

"And the pistol too," say the men.

Dritto loosens his belt and lets the pistol fall to the ground.

"Let's go," he says.

Now he is standing between the two men.

He turns round: "Our turn to fetch the rations is at two o'clock. Begin getting everything ready. At half-past three, two of our men must go on sentry duty, beginning from where the last night's roster broke off."

He turns round again and walks off between the two men.

CHAPTER TWELVE

PIN IS sitting all alone on a mountain crest; sheer away at his feet drop rocky slopes furry with bushes, and then valley folding into valley down to where black rivers coil in the depths. Long wisps of cloud are moving up the slopes and blotting out the scattered villages and trees.

Something irreparable has happened to Pin now — as irreparable as when he stole the pistol from the sailor, or left the men in the tavern, or escaped from prison. Never again will he be able to return to the detachment, never will he be able to go into action with them now. It is sad to be like him, a child in a world of grown-ups, always treated as an amusement or a nuisance; and never to be able to use those exciting and mysterious things, weapons and women, never to be able to take part in their games. But one day Pin will be grown-up too, and be able to behave really badly to everyone, revenge himself on those who have behaved badly to him; how Pin would like to be grown-up now, or rather not grown-up, but as he is yet admired and feared, a child and yet a leader of grown-ups on some marvellous enterprise.

Now he will leave these windswept unknown parts and go far away, back to his own kingdom in the river-bed, back to the magic spot where the spiders make their nests. Down there his pistol is buried, with that mysterious name; pee thirty-eight. With his pistol Pin will become a partisan all on his own, with no one to twist his arm till it nearly breaks, no one to send him off to bury dead hawks so that a man and woman can roll about together among alpenroses. He will do wonderful things, will Pin, always on his own; kill an officer, a captain, the captain who goes round with that bitch and spy of a sister. Then he will be respected by all the grown-ups, and they will want him to go into action with them; perhaps they will teach him how to handle a machine-gun. And Giglia will no longer say: "Sing us a song, Pin," just so that she can snuggle up against her lover; Giglia won't have lovers any more, and one day she will let her breast be touched by him, by Pin, that warm rosy breast under its man's shirt.

Now Pin is walking with long strides along the paths winding down the mountainside from the Pass of the Half-Moon; he has a long way to go. And as he walks along he begins to feel that his enthusiasm for those projects was forced, not genuine at all, that they were just fantasies which would never come about in reality, and that he would go on being a poor lost wandering child forever.

Pin walks for the whole day long. He passes places where lovely games could be played, with big white stones to jump about on and twisted trees to climb; he sees squirrels on the tops of pine-trees, snakes winding through the undergrowth, all good targets for stones. But Pin feels no desire to play any games, and goes on walking as hard as he can go, with the sadness clouding in his throat.

He passes a cottage and stops to ask for something to eat. It is inhabited by an old couple who keep goats. The two old folk greet him kindly, offer him chestnuts and milk, and talk about their sons who are all prisoners-of-war far away; then they sit round the fire and begin saying the Rosary, asking Pin to join in too.

But Pin is not used to dealing with people who are good and feels ill at ease — nor is he used to saying the Rosary; so while the old couple are murmuring away with closed eyes he quietly gets down from his chair and goes off.

That night he digs himself a hole in a haystack and sleeps in it; in the morning he presses on, into areas that are becoming more dangerous, infested by Germans. But Pin realises how useful it sometimes is to be a child, and how no one would believe him even if he said quite openly that he was a partisan.

At one point he finds the way barred by a block post. From some way off he can see Germans frowning at him under their helmets. Pin goes boldly up to them.

"My sheep," he says. "Have you seen my sheep?"

"Was?" The Germans can't understand.

"Sheep. She-e-e-p. Ba-a-a-a . . ."

The Germans laugh; they have understood. With that long hair and the mud coating him Pin might easily be a little shepherd-boy.

"I've lost a sheep," he whines. "It must have passed this

way, for sure. Where's it gone to?" And Pin nips under the barrier and walks on, calling out, "Ba-a-a-a . . ." "He's got away with that too.

The sea, which yesterday looked just a turbid mass of cloud on the edge of the sky, is now becoming a darkening strip of colour and then a great blue background to the hills and houses.

Pin reaches his own river bed. It's an evening with very few frogs about. Black midges are setting the water in the puddles aquiver. There, beyond the bamboos, begins the path of the spiders' nests, the magic place which only Pin knows. There he can weave strange spells, become a king, a god. He starts walking up the path, his heart in his mouth. Yes, there are the nests. But the earth is disturbed, some hand seems to have pased over it all, tearing up the grass, moving the stones, destroying the nests and breaking open their little doors; Pelle! Pelle knew the place; he's been here, with those lips of his slobbering with rage, scooped the loose earth out with his hands, pushed sticks into the tunnels and killed all the spiders one by one, looking for the pee thirty-eight pistol! Did he find it? Pin can no longer recognise the place; the stones he had laid are no longer there, the grass is torn out in handfuls. This should be the place though, the hole he scooped out for it is still there, but now it's full of earth and bits of stone.

Pin puts his head in his hands and sobs. No one will ever give him his pistol back now. Pelle is dead and did not have it among his weapons; where could he have put it, who could he have given it to? The pistol was the last thing Pin had in all the world; what is he to do now? He can't go back to the partisans; he has behaved too badly to all of them, Mancino, Giglia, Duke, Long Zena. There has been a round-up at the tavern and everyone there is deported or killed. The only one left is Frenchy Michel, in the Black Brigade. But Pin does not want to end up like Pelle, climbing up a long staircase waiting to be shot at. He is alone in all the world, is Pin.

*   *   *

The Dark Girl of Long Alley is trying on a new blue dress, when she hears a knock at the door. She listens; these days she is afraid of opening her door to people she doesn't know, when she's in her old home in the Alley.

"Who's there?"

"Open up, Rina. It's your brother, Pin."

Rina opens the door and her brother comes in, dressed in strange muddy clothes, with a shock of hair wider than his shoulders, filthy, ragged, his boots falling to bits, his cheeks clotted with dust and tears.

"Pin! Where on earth have you come from? Where have you been all this time?"

Pin enters without looking at her, and says hoarsely: "Now don't begin worrying me. I've been to places I wanted to go to. Have you anything to eat?"

The Dark Girl becomes all maternal: "Wait a minute and I'll get something ready. Sit down. How tired you look, poor Pin. You're lucky to have found me at home. I'm scarcely ever here nowadays. I live at the hotel now."

Pin begins chewing bread and a piece of German ersatz chocolate made with groundnuts.

"They treat you well, I see."

"Pin, I've been so worried about you! What have you been doing all this time? Being a vagabond, a rebel?"

"And you?" asks Pin.

The Dark Girl is spreading slices of bread with German ersatz jam and passing them to him.

"And what are you going to do now, Pin?"

"I don't know. Let me eat."

"Look here, Pin, you must try and be sensible. You know, at the place I work they need bright lads like you and could look after you well. There's no real work; just going round all day, watching people."

"Say, Rina, have you any weapons?"

"Me?"

"Yes, you."

"Well, I've got a pistol. I keep it with me because one never knows these days. Someone from the Black Brigade gave it to me."

Pin raises his eyes and swallows down the last mouthful. "Will you show it to me, Rina?"

The Dark Girl gets up. "Why are you so fixed on pistols? Didn't you have enough of them when you stole Frick's? This one is like Frick's. Here it is. Poor Frick, they've sent him over to the Atlantic coast."

Pin looks at the pistol, fascinated. It's a pee thirty-eight. His pee thirty-eight!

"Who gave it to you?"

"I told you, someone in the Black Brigade. A blond boy; he had such a cold. And without exaggeration he must have had at least seven different pistols on him. 'What d'you do with so many?' I asked. 'Give me one,' I said. But he didn't want to, however much I begged him. A mania for pistols, he had. Finally he gave me this one because it was in the worst condition. But it works quite well. 'What's this you're giving me,' I said, 'a cannon?' And he said, 'All right, then it's all in the family.' I wonder what he meant."

Pin is not even listening any more; he is turning his pistol over and over in his hand. Then he raises his eyes to his sister, hugging the pistol to his chest as if it were a doll, and says hoarsely, "Listen to me, Rina, this pistol's mine!"

The Dark Girl gives him a black look. "What's got hold of you? Have you become a rebel?"

Pin takes up a chair and flings it on the ground.

"Cow!" he shouts with all his strength. "Bitch! Spy!"

He thrusts the pistol into a pocket and bangs the door on his way out.

*   *   *

Outside it is already night. The Alley is deserted, like when he came. The shutters of the shops are up. There are shrapnel shelters against the walls, made of planks and sandbags.

Pin takes the path to the river-bed. He feels as if he were back at that night when he stole the pistol. Now he has his pistol, but everything is just as it was; he is alone in all the world, and lonelier than ever. And Pin's heart is overflowing with a single question, as it was that night: "What shall I do?"

He walks along the irrigation channels, weeping. First he cries silently then breaks out into loud sobs. There is no one coming towards him now, as there was before. Isn't there? No one? A big shadow is falling on a turn of the channel.

"Cousin!"

"Pin!"

These are enchanted places, where magical things always happen. The pistol is enchanted too, like a magic wand. And Cousin is also like a great magician, with his tommy-gun and his woollen cap, as he puts a hand on Pin's shoulder and asks: "Well, Pin, what are you doing down here?"

"I came to fetch my pistol. Look. A German naval pistol."

Cousin looks at it closely.

"Lovely. A P.38. Look after it carefully."

"And you, what are you doing here, Cousin?"

Cousin sighs, with that eternally regretful air of his, as if he were always doing some penance.

"I'm going to pay a visit," he says.

"These places are mine, down here. Magic places. Spiders make their nests here."

"Do spiders make nests, Pin?"

"This is the only place in the whole world where they do," explains Pin, "and I'm the only person who knows it. Then that Fascist Pelle came and mucked everything up. Would you like me to show you?"

"Yes, show me, Pin. Spiders' nests, just fancy."

Pin takes him by his big hand, soft and warm as bread.

"There, you see, here there were lots of doors into their little tunnels. That Fascist swine broke them all up. Here is a complete one still, d'you see?"

Cousin has knelt down nearby and is peering into the darkness. "Look, look, a little door that opens and shuts. And a tunnel inside. Is it deep?"

"Very deep," explains Pin, "with bits of grass stuck all round the sides. The spider is at the end."

"Let's light a match," says Cousin.

They both kneel down, side by side, watching the mouth of the tunnel by the light of the match.

"Here, throw the match inside," says Pin, "let's see if the spider comes out."

"Why, poor little thing?" says Cousin. "Don't you see how much harm has been done to them already?"

"Say, Cousin, d'you think they'll remake their nests?"

"Yes, I think so, if we leave them in peace."

"Shall we come back another time and see?"

"Yes, Pin, we'll pass by this way every month and have a look."

How wonderful it is to have found Cousin, who is interested in spiders' nests.

"Say, Pin."

"Yes, Cousin?"

"Say, Pin, there's something I want to tell you. I know you understand these things. You see, it's months and months since I've been with a woman. . . . You understand these things, Pin. Listen, they say that your sister . . ."

Pin is grinning his old grin; he is the grown-ups' friend,

is Pin; yes, he understands these things and is willing to help
out his friends about them when he can. "Hell, Cousin,
you'll be all right with my sister. I'll show you the way. D'you
know Long Alley? Well, it's the door after the carpenter's,
about half way up. Don't worry, you won't meet anyone in
the street. But be a bit careful with her. Don't say who you
are, nor that I sent you. Tell her you work at the 'Todt' and
are just passing through. Ha, Cousin, yet you're always talking against women. Go on, then, she's dark, my sister is, and
men like her a lot."

A slight smile passes over Cousin's big disconsolate features.

"Thank you, Pin. You're a real friend. I'll be back
soon."

"God, Cousin, are you taking your tommy-gun with you?"

Cousin passes a finger over his moustaches.

"Well, you see, I don't like going around unarmed."

Cousin seems so embarrassed about this that it makes
Pin laugh. "Here, take my pistol. Leave me the tommy-gun
and I'll keep guard over it."

Cousin puts down the tommy-gun, thrusts the pistol into
his pocket, then takes off his woollen cap and puts that into
his pocket too. Then he tries to tidy his hair with two fingers
wet with spittle.

"You're making yourself look your best, I see, Cousin.
You want to make an impression. Be quick, now, if you want
to find her at home."

"See you soon, Pin," says Cousin, and off he goes.

Now Pin is alone in the darkness, by the spiders' nests,
with the tommy-gun on the ground near him. But he is no
longer in despair. He has found Cousin, and Cousin is the
great friend he has sought for so long, the friend who is
interested in spiders' nests. Yet Cousin is like all other grown-
ups, with that mysterious desire for women, and now he has
gone to visit his sister and is embracing her on the unmade

bed. Thinking it over, Pin decides that it would have been nicer if Cousin had not thought of that, and stayed there instead looking at the spiders' nests a little longer, and made his usual remarks against women which Pin approved and understood so perfectly. Instead of which Cousin is like all other grown-ups; there's nothing to be done about it, Pin understands these things.

Shots, down in the Old Town. Who can it be? Patrols, perhaps, on their rounds. Shots, at night like that, are always frightening. Cousin was really rather rash to go alone into that nest of Fascists, for a woman. Pin is worried he may fall into the hands of a patrol, or find his sister's room full of Germans and get captured. Deep down, though, Pin feels that would be only just. What pleasure can he get from going with that hairy frog of a sister of his?

But if Cousin is captured, Pin would be all alone, alone with that tommy-gun which frightens him and he doesn't know how to handle. He hopes Cousin won't be captured, he hopes it with all his might, not because Cousin is the Great Friend he was looking for, no, he's not that any more, he's just a man like all the others, but because he is the last person Pin has left in all the world.

He needn't begin worrying, though, for some time, he must wait. Instead of which he now sees a shadow coming nearer, and there he is already.

"How ever were you so quick, Cousin, have you already done it?"

Cousin shakes his head with that disconsolate air of his.

"No. You know, I got disgusted and came away without doing anything."

"Hell, Cousin, you got disgusted?"

Pin is delighted. He really is the Great Friend, Cousin is, he understands everything; even how filthy women are.

Cousin puts the tommy-gun back on his shoulder and hands the pistol back to Pin.

They walk off into the country, with Pin holding Cousin's big soft calming hand.

The darkness is punctured with tiny spots of light; numberless fireflies are flickering over the hedges.

"Filthy creatures, women, Cousin . . ." says Pin.

"All of them . . ." agrees Cousin. "But they weren't always; now my mother . . ."

"Can you remember your mother, then?" asks Pin.

"Yes, she died when I was fifteen," says Cousin.

"Was she nice?"

"Yes," says Cousin, "she was nice."

"Mine was nice too," says Pin.

"What a lot of fireflies," says Cousin.

"If you look at them really closely, the fireflies," says Pin, "they're filthy creatures too, reddish."

"Yes," says Cousin, "I've never seen them looking so beautiful."

And they walk on, the big man and the child, into the night, amid the fireflies, holding each other by the hand.

THE END